JAIL BIRDS AND OTHERS

BOTSOTSO
PUBLISHING

Published by Botsotso Publishing 2004
P O Box 23910, Joubert Park, 2044
botsotso@artslink.co.za

Copyright © Muthal Naidoo 2004

ISBN 978-0-620-33399-3

Cover design and layout by Vivienne Preston

The publication of this book has been made possible by
a grant from the National Arts Council.

NATIONAL ARTS COUNCIL
OF SOUTH AFRICA

In the years that she was involved in theatre, Muthal Naidoo, a retired teacher, was an actor, director and playwright. Most of her work was done in Durban between 1977 and 1983.

Her plays include *We 3 Kings, Ikhayalethu* (originally *Coming Home*), *Masks, Of No Account, Nobody's Hero, Outside-In* and a number of short plays and revues. *Of No Account and Coming Home (Ikhayalethu)* were nominated for the Critics' Circle Award in Durban. In 1983 her revue *The Master Plan* - a satire based on the Tri-Cameral elections and proposals and performed at UDF meetings in the Durban area - was banned. *We 3 Kings* was published by the University of Durban-Westville in 1992. *Flight from the Mahabarath* was published by UCT in an anthology edited by Dr Kathy Perkins, *Black South African Women: An Anthology of Plays.* In 2002 *Outside-In* was published in an anthology by Rajendra Chetty entitled *South African Indian Writings in English.* In 2004, she published *A Little Book of Tamil Religious Rituals,* a concise book on Hinduism and the symbols and symbolic processes of Tamil rituals.

This book is dedicated to the late Seetha Ray.

Seetha Ray, younger sister of Muthal Naidoo, also a teacher, was involved in the Shah Theatre Academy in 1963 and 1964 as an actor and playwright.
She took up a teaching post in London in 1965. In 1969 she married and went to live in Calcutta. In 1972, with her husband and baby daughter, she emigrated to the USA where she began to write about her experiences in India. Her story *Meera* is included in this collection.
Seetha Ray died in 1993.

Acknowledgements

I am very grateful to Brenda George for her invaluable advice and constructive criticism of the manuscript.

Thank you to Allan Kolski Horwitz for his encouragement and support, to MPL A.R. Dawood for endorsing my application to the NAC for funding and to Carol Parsons for reading the first draft.

CONTENTS

The Intruder

She fixed an irate and accusing stare as she pointed a finger at the little old woman with straggly grey hair, who stared back at her equally irate and accusing. "Anusha, who is this old woman in my room," she shouted but there was no response. She hurried into the kitchen where Anusha was busy preparing her supper. "Anusha, come and see, there's an old woman in my room. She wants to steal my saris and jewellery."

"There's no one in your room, Ma."

"Come and see," she insisted.

"But, Ma," Anusha began to protest.

She came and stood right next to Anusha at the sink where she was washing the rice. "You must come and see. I don't know why you bring all these people here. They just come to steal my things. You don't care about your mother. Nobody cares about me. When I die, I will die alone."

Anusha set the bowl of rice down. "All right, Ma, come; let's go find this woman."

"She's in my room. What she's doing in my room?"

She led the way in and there was the old woman staring back at her again.

"You see," she exclaimed, pointing at the old woman, who pointed right back at her. And of all the cheek, she couldn't believe her eyes! "Look! Look! She brought her friend." She turned to Anusha in outrage. Then she turned back to the old woman. "What you want here? Get out of my room. This is my room. Don't bring your friends here."

But she could see that Anusha, who was murmuring, "All right, Ma," and pushing her into the living room, wasn't listening. Just because she was old, her daughter was treating her like an idiot. *Anusha mustn't think I'm a fool.*

"What you doing, Anusha? You left those people in my room. They will steal everything—all my saris and jewellery."

But Anusha, still not listening, was nudging her into a chair. "You wait here. I'm going to chase them away."

"I'll come too. I'll take my saris and jewellery from them."

But as she tried to get up, Anusha pushed her back in the chair.

"Don't worry, Ma. They won't take your things. I won't let them." When Anusha went into her bedroom, she got up quickly and watched her through a crack in the door. What was Anusha doing? What was she doing with that old blanket? Then Anusha called out, "Come and see, Ma. They've gone."

She went in and looked around – there was no one. *Where did she go?* She frowned at Anusha. *My daughter thinks she's very clever but she can't fool me. I don't know what she did with her, but I know that old woman is still here, somewhere, just waiting to steal my jewellery.*

When she was living with her son, Aru, and his wife, Kamala, her things used to go missing there too. She knew Kamala was stealing her things and telling lies about her to Aru. That's why he sent her away. Her son loved her but he sent her away, all because of that Kamala. Aru didn't believe her, his own mother; he believed his wife. Even though he knew that Kamala had tried to poison her. Ya, she gave her a plate of porridge with glass sticking out on top. She wasn't going to eat that. She ran right out of the house to show Devi what her daughter-in-law was doing to her. Devi, would believe her; her son didn't but her daughter would. Devi lived a few streets away and she knew how to get to her house. She ran out but when she got to the corner there were so many buses, they were making her dizzy. But she had to get to Devi so she didn't worry about the buses, she just ran. She heard brakes screeching and people shouting but she didn't stop. When she got to Devi's house, she banged on the door and pushed the offending plate under her daughter's nose. "Look, Devi," she exclaimed, "she's trying to kill me. See, she put glass in my porridge."

On another occasion, she saw Kamala in her room fiddling with the bedclothes. Kamala must have known that she kept her money under the mattress. When Kamala left her room, she stuffed the little money she had in a bag, and rushed out. She was taking her money to Devi for safekeeping. *But the world is full of thieves.* As she was hurrying to the corner, somebody grabbed her bag and when she wouldn't let go, he hit her and as she tried to get away from him, she didn't see the bus coming. Then she heard Kamala screaming and pulling her to the pavement. She fought with Kamala right there on the street but Kamala just held on to her and made her go back in the house.

She was so angry, she went into her room and just sat on the bed. She was not going to say one word to her daughter-in-law. She would wait for Aru. When Aru came home, she told him how his wife had tried to steal her money. And what did that Kamala say? She was just changing the bedclothes. What a liar! Then that Kamala told Aru that she had nearly caused a big accident on the street and that somebody had hit her and stolen her bag with her money and that she could have been killed. She had screamed, "Lies, lies, all lies. Your wife is trying to kill me. She took my money." She was going to hit Kamala but her heart was beating so fast and there was such a pain in her head, she just sat down right there on the floor. The next thing she knew, the doctor was there. He gave her something and Aru took her to her bed.

After that Aru sent her away. He said she wasn't safe in his house because of the buses and the people. But she realised he didn't love his mother anymore. His wife had turned him against her. So he sent her to stay with Anusha, far away from him and Devi. She didn't know this place. She didn't know anybody in this place. She couldn't visit anyone. This was like a jail. Anusha, her youngest daughter, was a caterer and people were in and out of her house ordering samoosas or cakes or contracting her services for weddings, birthday parties and so on. *I know she wants me to help her because she can't cook like me. But I won't. She must stop this cooking business. Too many people come here. There's always somebody in the sitting room and in the kitchen. This place is like a machenie.*

Her saris and jewellery were not safe in this house so when people came to collect their orders, she followed close behind, watching them like a hawk. When they left, she would warn Anusha, "People come to see what you have so they can steal all your goods. I saw someone walk out with a bundle." Then she would go into her room and begin counting her saris and jewels again.

And today she had found that old woman in her room. *Anusha says she's gone but I don't believe her.* She looked around, opened the wardrobe, looked under the bed but she didn't see anyone. She couldn't make head or tail of it. *Better count my saris and jewels.* Then she saw the blanket on the wall. That was the blanket she had spied through the door. What was it doing on the wall? She crept over, pulled it down and gasped at what she saw. The old lady! She was still here.

Mother dropped down onto her bed shaking with terror. The

tabla in her chest began to beat out a very loud and arhythmic *tala*. She pressed her hands over her heart to stop the dreadful drumming. When Anusha called out to her that supper was ready, she just sat there paralysed. Suddenly Anusha was next to her. She looked very frightened and said she was going to call the doctor. After the doctor's visit, Anusha put her to bed and sat with her until she fell asleep.

The next morning, when she got up, she searched the room but the old lady was nowhere to be found. She didn't know what to think. And she couldn't ask Anusha. Her daughter had acted very strangely, pretending that the old woman wasn't there. *Anusha mustn't think I'm a fool; I saw her with my own eyes. Why Anusha is hiding this old woman in my room?* Then it struck her. *Of course! They want my saris and jewels. If only I can go to Devi and tell her. Why I came to live here, in this train station, I don't know.*

She looked around and frowned. There was something different about the room but she couldn't figure it out. She was staring at the blank wall with the screw holes when Anusha came in and began scolding her. "Ma, why are you up? You must rest. Please, go back to bed." Anusha took hold of her but she pushed her daughter away roughly.

"No. I want to eat. When you going to cook chicken curry? I want chicken curry."

"But, Ma," Anusha began, "don't you want some nice porridge?"

"I want chicken curry. Why you don't want to give me chicken curry? I'm starving in this house. I don't know why you brought me here? You never cared about me. I want my son. I want to stay with my Aru."

"All right, Ma. I'm going to cook some chicken curry. But it will take time. Won't you have some porridge first?"

"You don't care about me. Nobody cares about me. When I die, I will die alone."

She let Anusha lead her into the dining room and set a cup of tea in front of her. While her daughter was busy in the kitchen preparing her breakfast, she wandered into Anusha's room. Suddenly, a loud gasp escaped her and she dropped her cup, splashing tea over her slippers and on the carpet. The old lady was here, in Anusha's room! She was standing there pointing an accusing finger and looking at her in horror. Anusha came running in and began pulling her away from the dressing table, but she couldn't take her eyes off the old woman.

"Why you hiding this old woman here? Who she is to you? You look after her better than you look after me. Now you take her in your room." There was that tabla again, pounding out its dreadful beat. She couldn't stay in this room. She stumbled out and made for the garden. Anusha came after her and tried to take her by the arm to lead her back to her room. But she pushed her daughter off. "Don't pretend you worried about me. Go away. I don't want to live in this house anymore. Not with that old woman here."

"Ma, I am going to chase her away. I don't want her here. Please come inside and rest. Come and eat your breakfast."

"Why you got that woman in your house? She wants to kill me."

"No, Ma. I won't let her touch you. I am going to chase her away. Please come inside." She was exhausted and eventually went in to lie down. Later that day, she got up and went into Anusha's room to look for the old lady but she couldn't find her. *I know she's hiding here somewhere. Anusha mustn't think she's clever. I know she got that old woman here.* She decided not to say anything but she would be vigilant.

During the next few days, while Anusha was busy with preparations for a wedding reception at the temple, she quietly alternated counting her saris and jewels with her search for the old woman. Every now and then she would see Anusha carrying stuff – looked like pictures – to the garage. What was she doing? She didn't understand her daughter and she didn't know why Anusha was taking better care of a strange old woman rather than her own mother. *She's starving me but she's cooking chicken curry for that old woman. She doesn't care about me, only about that old thief. I know she's hiding her somewhere. But I'm going to find her.*

On Sunday, Anusha wanted her to go to the wedding with her but she refused.

"But Ma, you will be alone. Who will give you your food?"

She said nothing. Her daughter didn't care about her. Nobody cared about her. She heard Anusha telephoning around but no one wanted to come and be with her. Then she saw Anusha going next door to her neighbour. *She's going to ask those two children from next door. They just come and sit in front of the TV for hours. How they can sit like that? Why their mother don't buy a TV? Then they can sit in their own house.*

She saw the teenagers, Krishna and Kanthi, coming back with Anusha and decided not to come out of her room. When Anusha came to say she was leaving, she didn't respond.

After a while, she decided to check on her saris and jewels. When she was sure that nothing was missing, she peeped into the living room and saw Krishna and Kanthi in front of the television. *Hmph! There they sitting. Like statues.* She shook her head and went off to look for the old woman. She didn't find her in the house and decided that she must be outside somewhere. She opened the back door and slipped out.

* * *

Krishna and Kanthi had settled down in front of the television and were oblivious to the world around them. When their movie ended, Krishna reminded Kanthi to warm up the meal that Anusha had prepared for her mother. While his sister was in the kitchen, he laid the table and then went back to fiddle with the TV. Kanthi dished out and went to call Mother. But Mother was not in her room. Kanthi looked in Anusha's room, but Mother wasn't there. The backdoor was open so she looked in the yard, but there was no one there.

"Krishna, I can't find *Parti.* Have you seen her?"

"Maybe she's in the garden," Krishna suggested. Kanthi went to the front door and looked out.

"She's not in the garden. Where can she be?" Kanthi was frowning.

"She must be around somewhere. You haven't looked properly."

"She's not here. I can't find her."

"Oh man, what you so worried for? She must be here somewhere." His sister scowled at him. "Okay, okay, I'll help you look for her. I'm sure we'll find her." They searched the house together but Mother wasn't to be found.

"Do you think she's at our house?" Kanthi looked worried.

"But she never comes over, not even with aunty Anusha."

"Then where is she?" Kanthi became alarmed. "What if she went out on the street? We must tell Ma." They were hoping against hope that they would find *Parti* at their house even though they knew their mother would be angry with them for neglecting the old lady. But

Parti was not there and their mother, who had heard the stories of Anusha's mother wandering about on the streets when she lived with Aru, began to panic. She and the children jumped into the car and went off to scour the neighbourhood.

*   *   *

But mother had not left the premises.

When she slipped out of the back door, into the yard, she found the garage gaping open, it had struck her immediately. *That's where Anusha is hiding her.* She knew, without the shadow of a doubt, that she would find the old woman in there. So she picked up a spade that was against the wall and advanced on the garage. She was going to get rid of the old witch once and for all. She peered into the garage but couldn't see her. *She's very cunning; she knows I'm coming.* She moved in cautiously. *Where's the old crone?* She turned around and gasped. There she was against the wall. The drumbeats began to pound in her ears. The arhythmia filled her with rage and power. She lifted the spade; her every intention was to bring it down on the head of the thieving old woman confronting her.

But as she raised her weapon, so did the old woman. Her eyes, murderous and compelling, filled her with terror and paralysed her in her tracks. The old woman knew she had the advantage. She sprang and delivered a tremendous blow to the cranium. Mother felt her skull crack open and she fell limp and lifeless to the ground.

Mihloti

Sitting on the patio, busy with her crochet work, Mihloti presented a picture of quiet domesticity, but her heart was aching. She had been gravely ill but that wasn't it. It was her husband, Robert. The day they took her to the hospital, he saw it. Robert, sitting under the tree on the lawn, saw James and Mary carrying her to the car. *James, he hold me. He put me in the car. He* (Robert) *was only sitting at the shadow under the tree. He didn't say one word. He didn't ask, 'How are you? Where are you going?'* Sick as she was, she knew that he had only come there for money and wasn't interested in what was happening to her.

Robert had not been near her when she was in the hospital and hadn't come even now she was back and recuperating. He was her husband but he wasn't taking care of her. He was leaving it all to James and Mary. And he shouldn't do that. They were not family. They treated her like family but she was their helper. They were from Cape Town and had been here only three years. Why should they look after her? *I have a husband . . . But men, they can't look after a woman. They think, 'I am a man, you are a woman, so be down.' But not if you love someone. I can't be down.* Sitting there, working on her crochet, she made up her mind. *I'll forget him.*

In Johannesburg, where they had met, he had been a good man, a soft man. He had come to the house, where she was a domestic, looking for work and her madam had employed him as a gardener. He came there two, three times a week and she had to give him his tea and lunch. They became friendly and she could see that he was interested in her. Her madam disapproved, "I don't want to see you with that man.' But she knew he loved her very much and she loved him very much. So they decided to get married and go back to his village in the homeland.

When they arrived at Sekhunyane Village, she was shocked to find that he already had a wife and children. When she had confronted him, he had simply shrugged it off, A man can have many wives. *How could he think that? He was a Christian!* Mihloti was ashamed and hurt. She had immediately thought of divorce. Zodwa, his first wife, had tried to comfort her, 'No problem, it's Okay. Don't worry. Here at Gazankulu we do that.' Mihloti was horrified but Robert ignored her feelings and set her up in her own rooms, opposite Zodwa's hut. She didn't know what to do. She had left her job and family in Johannesburg and had no one up here. She was trapped. What could she do? God had given her this cross to bear. So she stayed, became the second wife and bore his children.

Ashley, James and Mary's two-and-a-half year old, jumped into her lap and brought her back to the present quite abruptly. He had fallen off his tricycle and needed comforting. She cradled him in her arms for a few minutes and then he was off again to conquer the world. This was a happy home, not like hers.

Though it was over twenty years ago, Mihloti still couldn't wipe out the shame of her marriage and she had never made friends with Zodwa, who was a constant reminder of her disgrace. Robert knew the women didn't get on but he didn't care. At first, Mihloti, who had committed herself to him, had not been able to understand how he could love two women. It was only after she found a job at the campus that she came to understand that he didn't love her. When she began earning, he gave up all responsibility for her and she couldn't ask him for anything. He would say, 'I have no money now. You work, use your money.' So she had furnished her rooms from her wages. All the stuff in her house at Sekhunyane was hers. He had given her nothing. Finally she understood; he had married her so she would support him. Still, she stayed with him. She had children to take care of and to provide for until they were old enough to take care of themselves and go their own ways.

When she started working for James and Mary, they offered her a room in their house and she came to live on the college campus. Robert took to visiting her there, always for money. He came two or three times a week. When she became ill, he stopped coming so regularly. Just before she went to hospital, he told her he was tired of her being sick. He didn't want a woman who was sick all the time.

But it was unusual for Mihloti to be ill. She was a robust and active woman and this illness had taken her by surprise. At first she had simply dismissed it and even though she looked and felt awful, had insisted on getting on with her duties. But the pain in her stomach had become more than she could bear and she was forced to seek medical aid. She went from doctor to doctor in the township and came away each time with pills that had no effect on her whatever. Not even the inyanga was able to help her.

When her condition continued to deteriorate, James and Mary's concern grew into alarm. Little Ashley, who called her Toto, he couldn't say *Gogo*, also knew that something was wrong. When he was not able to share her bed anymore, he became naughty and difficult to control. Then came the morning when she could not get out of bed and Ashley, who was always up first, came in and found her lying there, unable to speak. The little boy got a terrible fright and ran off to his mother, shouting, *"Mani* (Shangaan for Mummy), *Mani*, Toto, Toto."

After a few minutes, Mary came into her room, took one look at her and ran out again. When she came back, James was with her. She didn't have the strength to protest when they wrapped her in a blanket and carried her out to the car. They were surprised to see Robert in the garden. They greeted him and after they put her in the car, James went over to tell him that they were taking Mihloti to the doctor. When James came back to the car, she could see that Robert had said nothing. James moved Ashley, who was banging on the hooter, into the passenger's seat, and they had to endure his screaming as he fought with his father who was struggling to buckle him up. Ashley usually sat in the back with Mihloti but Mary had got in with her and was holding her. They drove off leaving Robert smoking silently under the tree.

James and Mary took Mihloti to Dr. Schoeman from their church. But like Dr Khosa, Dr. Shimati and others, he simply found that she had an upset tummy and dispensed the usual pills. When they came out of the surgery, James looked at Mary and shook his head. Mihloti tried to tell them to take her home; there was nothing more they could do but she was too weak and they weren't listening.

"This won't do. We've been hearing this same story for weeks now."

Mary was frowning. "Well, we could take her to Duiwelskloof. You know, Shanta is always raving about her doctor at the private medical centre there." Mihloti knew Shanta. She was a lecturer too and often came to visit them.

James nodded, "Let's do it."

Mihloti tried to protest but Mary hushed her and they drove off. Mihloti didn't want them to make her their responsibility. They were Coloured people and they weren't rich. They had come to work in Giyani and had inherited her with the house. She had worked for the lecturers who had occupied the house before them. James and Mary were very good people and Mihloti was happy with them. Then Ashley was born. Mary had told her she couldn't have children but within a year of being in Giyani, she had fallen pregnant. Mihloti could see she was shocked. She and James were studying for some high degree and they hadn't put away money for children. But Mary was so happy. Mihloti was happy too: a woman isn't a woman without children. She immediately began knitting baby clothes and Mary had laughed saying, "You are going to spoil this child." Mihloti had replied, "I'm his *Gogo*. I must look after him." From that time, she knew that they had to be very careful with their money. So she didn't want to be a burden on them.

But when she fell sick they took charge of her without any hesitation - just like family. They rushed her to Duiwelskloof, to the medical centre there and asked for Dr De Villiers. They did not have to wait long and when the doctor came, he took one look at Mihloti and ushered her into his rooms right away. While he was examining her, she could see from his face that it was something bad. Then he went out to talk to James and Mary. Mihloti tried to get up to tell them not to worry, she would manage, but the pain was so bad that she just collapsed on the examination table.

When she opened her eyes, she found Dr de Villiers trying to wake her up to tell her she had to go for an operation right away and before she knew what was happening they were wheeling her to the theatre. Afterwards Mary told her it was an ectopic pregnancy. She didn't know what that was and Mary had explained that the baby, foetus she called it, had got stuck in the fallopian tube and was dead and decomposing. Such a horrible thing! How she had cried. And she didn't know how James and Mary were going to manage; they had signed for everything and that meant they had to pay. She prayed to God to help them. They were good people; they went to church every Sunday, so they were not alone. God was with them.

But it broke her heart to think about Robert. He had been a good man - really a very good man. It was when he got the *bakkie* that he came to no good. He started coming home late, started shouting at her and demanding money. It was that *bakkie*. He couldn't stay in one place; he had to be moving all the time. And he started looking for other women.

She examined the pattern of her crochet work and shook her

head. Just as she had denied her illness, she had also denied his neglect and philandering. But his indifference - he hadn't visited her once in the three weeks that she was in hospital - finally broke something inside her and as traditional respect for him as a husband began to dissipate, she felt herself falling into an abyss. No longer bound by a sense of loyalty, negative thoughts took free rein and she became unhappier than she had ever been.

She hated herself for all her excuses, for tolerating the first wife and ignoring the fact that he had a girlfriend, a Zimbabwean, who lived in Kremetart. The affair had been going on for a long time but she had persistently looked the other way even though she knew he was taking money from her for his girlfriend. How could she have ended up in a marriage like this? Just like her mother? She had promised herself it would never happen to her. Her daddy had had another woman. When he died, they got nothing - all the furniture, all the money, went to the other woman. And here she was, even worse off than her mother.

Soon after she had moved into her room at James' house, Robert started taking his girlfriend to Sekhunyane. Early one morning, when Mihloti went to the village to fetch some of her things, she found them there; he was sleeping with this woman *on her bed, in her house.* Choking with fury and disgust, she had wanted to divorce him on the spot. Instead, she had confronted the woman; asked her why she hadn't taken him to her place. The woman had laughed in her face. She was an older woman but she had money. So he was happy with her and when Mihloti was in hospital, this woman took him on a visit to Zimbabwe.

After her discharge from the hospital, Mihloti had insisted that James send for Robert. He worked as a driver in one of the government departments and she wanted him to pay the medical bills. When Robert eventually came, he paid a cursory visit to tell Mihloti he couldn't help out; he had no money. Mihloti knew he was lying; he had been paid the day before. His money was probably going to the girlfriend; she knew Zodwa wasn't getting anything. She never got anything; she always went to her mother for money. When she came back, Robert would accuse her of having a boyfriend. Then he would beat her up so badly that she couldn't go anywhere because she looked a sight. Mihloti couldn't understand why Zodwa always came back to Robert. Why did she stay? Why did she stay? Why did she stay? The question buzzed around in her head like a mosquito.

Mihloti put her work down. She didn't want to think about this anymore. She looked up and watched Ashley, who had abandoned his tricycle and was chasing barbets on the lawn. But the buzzing in her head wouldn't stop.

At Mihloti's final check-up, Dr De Villiers, who had guessed at James and Mary's financial situation, told James not to worry - the centre had found a way to absorb the costs. That was good news and Mihloti had felt great relief. Though she was very grateful to Mary, James and the doctor, they were not family; there was no vital connection to them. The connection had been to Robert. And what had he given her? A dead baby that had become rotten inside of her. He had given her a dead, rotting baby! That was his gift to her. She would have died if it had not been for James and Mary. Why had she stayed, and stayed and stayed? She was no better than Zodwa. She *had to* forget him.

She sat there for a long time staring into the distance. Then quietly and deliberately, she conjured up Robert's image and strangled it until it became a dead, rotting thing. Then she tore it out of her system; tore it out by the roots and left a chasm inside where her traditional beliefs had been. She had cut herself loose and was floating free. She was free now, free - without a family. And the pain she felt was worse than the sickness that had been inside her. Without family she was nothing A person is a person through other people; she was no longer a person. When she died, she would join the walking dead. She stared with blank eyes at the abyss of meaninglessness that life had become.

Suddenly Ashley was in her lap again. "Toto, Toto, come and see. Mopani worms. Pretty! Come, come." And as she walked with him, his little hand in hers, she began to laugh. What a fool she was. She had not been a person with Robert. With Robert, she had walked among the dead. But here, she was Ashley's Toto.

Meera

Like a huge iron monster the train roared into Howrah station, Calcutta. It squealed to a stop and spat out its passengers onto the platform. Red-shirted porters rushed forward to carry luggage to and from the train.

"Come on, let's get in before all the seats are taken," Shomir urged Meera, who squeezed her way in with the crowd and managed to get a place by the window. Shomir was helping the porter to put their suitcases on the rack above the window, when a big, fat woman flopped down on the seat beside Meera. Shomir quickly paid the porter and sat down opposite his wife.

As the train slid out of the station, she fidgeted with the border of her sari. How thankful she felt to be sitting next to an open window. She could look out and watch the trees slipping past against the clear blue sky. She could avoid the inquisitive gaze of the other passengers. Most of all she could avoid looking at Shomir - her husband. How strange the word sounded. Was she really married to him - and going on a honeymoon? Two weeks seemed a long time to spend with someone she didn't even know. She stole a quick glance at him. He was smoking a cigarette and gazing lazily out of the window. She hadn't realized before that he smoked.

Turning once more to the window, Meera tried to concentrate on the scene outside, but she was acutely aware of Shomir, sitting across from her. The day that she first met him was clearly imprinted on her mind.

It was on a Tuesday, 17 July 1970, exactly twenty days ago. Rain had been falling steadily all morning. Her mother had come into her room. She put her arm around Meera and confided to her, "We are expecting some visitors this evening. A young man and his family are coming to take a look at you, and if they are pleased, they may make a proposal of marriage."

"But you and father will refuse it, won't you? Just like you did the others."

"I don't think so. You've just passed your M.A. It's time you were married, don't you think?"

"Why do I have to get married? Don't you want me anymore?" Meera had burst out, clenching her hands in fear.

"Of course we do. It's because we want to see you comfortably settled and married into a good family, that we are keen on this match. Your uncle knows these people, the son has just returned from England after spending three years there."

"How do I know if I'll like him?" Meera had demanded.

"Don't worry, if your father and I are impressed with him, I am sure you will be too. If we aren't satisfied, we'll refuse the proposal. After all, we do want you to be happy."

"But I'm quite happy here with you," Meera had said.

Her mother had laughed, "Come now, be a good girl and find something pretty to wear for this evening - maybe your green silk sari, and don't sulk."

After she had left, Meera had thought about what her mother had said. She knew that she would not disobey her parents because she loved them too much. She had always been a dutiful daughter and would do what was expected of her, even if she didn't agree with them at times.

How nervous Meera had been that evening as she sat close to her mother, her trembling hands folded in her lap. Mrs. Banerjee and her eldest daughter had asked her so many questions, "Can you sing? Do you play any musical instrument?"

"Yes." "No." She had answered in monosyllables, her voice sticking to her throat. Shomir had spoken to her father at the other end of the room. She had been overcome with shyness and had not looked at him once.

Next to her, the fat lady coughed loudly breaking into Meera's reverie. Startled, she looked inside the train and her eyes met Shomir's. He smiled at her, but she did not respond. Instead, she turned to the window, but not without noting how attractive he was and what a nice suit he was wearing - dark blue.

She didn't remember what he wore at the wedding or the reception. They had been surrounded by relatives all the time. Even this morning, what a big crowd had been waiting to see them off on their honeymoon. Meera thought about it again. How she had clung to her mother and wept.

"I don't want to go, Ma, I'm afraid. Please let me go home with you," she had begged.

But her mother had whispered, "Hush, my child, you are married now. You must go with your husband and be a good wife. I will miss you too." Her eyes had filled with tears as she bid Meera good-bye.

In the taxi, Shomir had tried to console her. "You'll like Digha," he had ventured. "It's not so crowded at this time of the year. I guess people don't want to be caught in the Monsoon rains." But Meera had sat silently, looking out of the window and dabbing her eyes with her handkerchief from time to time.

She felt a little foolish now, as she thought of her behaviour this morning. *What must Shomir think of her?* she wondered unhappily. *Did he think she was childish?* In spite of feeling uneasy at being with him, Meera was experiencing a kind of excitement, too, which was so new to her. She didn't know why, but it was important to her to know that he approved of her.

An hour later, the train pulled into Karakpur station. They sat at a table and sipped hot tea in the station restaurant while they waited for the bus to Digha.

"Tired?" Shomir asked gently.

"No," she lied, staring into her cup.

"We'll have a good rest when we get to Digha, " he smiled kindly. Toying nervously with her cup, Meera did not answer.

As Shomir left to see if the bus had arrived, Meera watched him furtively. How tall he was - at least six feet. She liked the way he walked - with an easy confident stride.

During the long bus journey they sat together; Meera was tired of looking through windows. Self-consciously she played with her gold bangles. After a while Shomir said, "Look through the window."

The trees and bushes had given way to the sandy beach. Soon the blue-green ocean came into full view. A little gasp of pleasure escaped Meera's lips as she took it in. She had never been to the sea-side before.

Moments later the bus stopped. As she climbed out, the wind caught at her rosy silk sari, exposing her painted toenails and slender feet in their red sandals. Using both arms, Meera held down her billowing sari as she walked towards the white, two-storeyed hotel with a neon sign over the entrance which read "Aloka." Shomir joined her after taking care of their luggage. They walked up the black stone stairs to their bedroom. Shomir closed the door, took off his coat, and flung himself down on the bed. "Phew, that feels good."

Meera looked at him, then at the other bed. She wanted to lie down, too, but she felt awkward with him there. She had always had a room to herself at home.

"Shall I order some lunch for us up here? I'm starving aren't you?"

"I think I'll have a shower first," Meera murmured. She felt so hot and sweaty after all that travelling. Her mouth was unusually dry, too. How self-conscious she felt as she walked to pick up her suitcase. But Shomir was there before her.

"Let me do that for you. It's quite heavy," he said, putting it on the bed. Then he turned towards Meera. Cupping his hands around her face, he kissed her on the lips. She looked at him for a second, her brown eyes wide with surprise. No one had ever done that to her before. She rushed out of the room and stood gripping the white balcony. The sea stretched out in front of her. A fresh breeze fanned her burning face. She felt a slight movement behind her. Shomir had come out. He lit a cigarette.

"I'm sorry if I upset you just now."

.She could hear concern in his voice. "Would you like to go down to the beach after lunch?"

Meera smiled slowly and nodded.

Later, they lazed on the sunlit beach teasing tiny little crabs which sidled cautiously out of their holes in the sand. When Meera or Shomir gently threw pebbles at them, they scuttled back into their holes, only to venture out again a little later. How Meera and Shomir laughed when a big wave caught them unawares and splashed them.

Meera was surprised to find that she was enjoying herself so much. Shomir was good company, too. He told her about England. "People are very polite there. They don't shove and push to get into a bus or theatre, like they do here."

"Why did you leave?" she asked shyly.

"I got homesick. I missed the crowds in the streets, my family, my friends and the sunshine." He smiled at her, "Now that I know you, I'm even happier that I came back."

Meera felt herself blushing. She looked towards the sea. The blood was rushing through her veins just like the waves rushing towards the shore. She didn't feel afraid anymore, but she did feel her body tingle like ice one minute and burn like fire the next. It must be the sea air, she rationalized to herself, I've heard people say that it affects one this way.

That evening after dinner, they strolled along the beach. Day became night. The water turned from blue-green to a dark mysterious presence. Big clouds were massing in the sky.

"It looks as if it might rain," Shomir murmured, "Let's go back."

Once they were safely back in their room, Shomir asked suddenly, "You don't feel unhappy anymore, do you? I mean being here alone with me?"

"Oh, no I - I ...," But Meera's voice trailed off into silence. She couldn't explain how she felt to Shomir. She even found it difficult to explain to herself.

Shomir came over to her. He tilted her face up so that their eyes met. "I'm going to kiss you again," he warned "Promise you won't run away this time."

"I promise." Meera heard her voice say with an eagerness she could not believe.

A new Meera seemed to be in control of her, someone she did not recognize - someone who appeared to be completely unpredictable.

Not Your Car!

Three young men surrounded the car in the schoolyard. Parvathy, wondering what they wanted, was about to ask when she saw the gun and instantly turned into ice. The leader yanked open the door and motioned her out. But she was frozen, mesmerised by the gun, which was hissing at her, "Get out, this is not your car! This is not your car!" Someone grabbed her and pushed her out. Lying on the ground, she saw the three agents of the syndicate jump in and drive off. Then all the statues around her thawed and everyone was running about.

Parvathy, still staring in the direction of her car's dusty wake, was only vaguely aware of Mrs Shabangu, a member of staff, helping her up. Parvathy couldn't believe how eagerly Kogila, her Toyota, had gone off with the repossession squad. She could have stalled? *But she's never stalled.* It was devastating to hear Kogila in the distance, her motor roaring jubilantly, "Free at last! Free at last! I am off into the Great Unknown. Goodbye Parvathy and good riddance! Don't try to find me. I'm not your car anymore." Parvathy was shocked that Kogila, caught up in the excitement of the moment, could just race off like that. How ungrateful! Parvathy had provided her with a wonderful life, safe and secure. She was never required to go on long arduous journeys into perilous territory and she spent a good deal of her time relaxing in the garage. What more did she want? Adventure, excitement, thrills? What nonsense! But she had to admit; Kogila was a spirited little car. Was it possible she was bored with driving to the store to buy Parvathy's favourite ginger jellies?

Parvathy knew that cars cooperate completely with hijackers; that is why owners never get them back. Like Kogila, they imagine that they are living in dreadful slavery and actually court the attention of hijackers. Parvathy couldn't believe that Kogila, at the mature age of six years, wanted adventure. She was just a basic little car without even a clock or radio but Parvathy knew she envied the big luxury models that flaunt their speed, their radios, speakers, telephones and air-conditioning. *Perhaps Kogila despises me because I don't have much money. Perhaps I have been too selfish, thinking only of myself. I know she hates that internal gear lock that fits like a garrotte and maybe she's ashamed of the alarm system that goes off at all hours and mainly in the garage. I should have got it fixed.* In her mind's eye she could see Kogila laughing, "And what good are they? I have been freed in spite of them." *But Kogila was dizzily speeding off, probably to a chop shop.*

She looked up and found herself surrounded by the concerned faces of the teachers. She had come on her usual Tuesday morning call to Nelson Mandela Primary to deliver jerseys and socks, her knitting club's contribution to children in the informal settlement. She had greeted all the teachers, deposited her box in the staff room and got into her car ready to drive off when Kogila was taken from her. No! When Kogila had abandoned her! She had run off and left her stranded. Tears rolling down her cheeks, Parvathy could only murmur, "She's gone, my Kogila, she's gone! What am I going to do?"

Parvathy who was being comforted by Mrs Shabangu, felt her stiffen. Huge shock written all over her face, she wanted to know, "Dear Lord, was there someone in the car? Who is this Kookalia? Your daughter?"

"No, no, no. Kogila, you know, my car. Mind you, she is like a daughter. She goes everywhere with me. What am I going to do? I am so dependent on her. What am I going to do?"

Mrs Shabangu gave her a strange look, took her into the staff room and made her a big cup of tea. "Did they get your handbag too?" When Parvathy nodded, she asked, "What did you have in there?"

"My ID, bankcard, pensioner's card and fifty rands. All gone, with my Kogila." Her hands were trembling and tea spilled into the saucer. She put the cup down, covered her face and began sobbing again. She felt so ashamed. How could she be blubbering like this? But every time she thought of Kogila she couldn't help herself. "Oh God, my Kogila is gone. What am I going to do without her?" Parvathy felt stupid to be breaking down like this, especially when Mrs Shabangu was being so kind, calling the bank, giving them all the details and securing her accounts.

"How am I going to get home? My keys. They took all my keys. I won't be able to get into my house."

Just then the Principal, Mr Sithole, put his head round the staff room door. "The police are here. They're waiting for you outside." He led Parvathy out and helped her climb the high step into the police van. All the way to the local police station, she couldn't stop mumbling, "Kogila, Kogila, Kogila." At the police station, she told her sad story of abandonment to the sergeant at the desk, then to a detective in his office, but they didn't care about Kogila's betrayal. They only wanted a description of 'the car' and as Parvathy lovingly dwelt on the little dents, the scratch on the windscreen, the missing hub cab, the front bumper that had come loose, she kept losing control. The detective, who for some reason couldn't look her in the eye, got up and left her there in the office.

A young man, sitting at another of the desks, looked very dejected. Perhaps he would listen to her story. Tearfully she ventured, "Have you been hijacked too?"

The young man turned an agitated face to her. "No. Somebody break in my shack and steal all my things." He shook his head. "I buy this shack so I can have my own place. Then I buy music centre and CD's. Cost me two thousand. That no-good Jabavu. He's watching all the time He's the one. He rob me. I know it. He don't work, just sit around and wait. When the people go for work, he break in and steal. I know it's him. I seen the tekkie marks on the side. His tekkies. I know that. I ask him about his tekkies and he say he didn't wear them that day. But I know it's him. If they don't do anything, I will. He mustn't think he's safe. I will get him. I didn't go for work today. I come here to report." His distress was obvious. "I lose one day's pay." He sat there shaking his head.

Glad that he had finished, Parvathy gave a little sob and burst out, "Kogila...," but before she could tell him her sad story, his detective came in and they went off together. She sank back in her chair and waited. She waited a long time but nobody came back, not even her detective. Haunted by visions of Kogila's smiling face flying off into the distance, she gave one foghorn blast after another into her tissues. When she couldn't bear it any longer, she stumbled out into the dim corridor and back to the reception area wailing, "Kogila, Kogila, Kogila." There everyone looked at her strangely. Nobody wanted to help her. Some of them stood about laughing and others rudely told her to be quiet. When the sergeant who had taken her statement came back to his desk, she went straight to him and when he saw her in front of him again, he quickly sent out a call to the policemen who had brought her to the station. When they came in, they were very kind, making sure she had her case number for the insurance company before they took her home. But she had no keys and couldn't get into her house, so she went next door to her neighbour, Mulligay.

Mulligay took one look at her distraught face and burst out, "What's wrong, A*athè?*"

"Kogila, she left me." To her shame, Parvathy began to cry again. Mulligay gathered Parvathy to her and cradled her in her arms. "What happened? You look terrible. Come inside and tell me all about it?" She took Parvathy into the kitchen, made tea and sat down with her at the little table. As she recounted the events again, Parvathy began to feel a rage building up inside her. After all she had done for Kogila, to be cast aside like this? She was amazed when Mulligay, who had completely missed the point of her story, began to scold her, "How many times I told you not to go there alone? How many times I told you how dangerous it is? You lucky to be alive." When Mulligay's daughter, Sundari, walked in with her four-year old son, Vasi, Mulligay jumped up. "Aunty Parvathy was hijacked! At gunpoint! Isn't it terrible? She's so lucky they didn't kill her."

Vasi ran up to Parvathy. *"Parti,* they hi-jack you? With a gun? Big gun like this?" He indicated with his hands. "What did you do? Did you fight them?"

"Don't be silly, Vasi. You can't fight someone with a gun." His mother turned apologetic eyes on Parvathy.

But Vasi was adamant. "I would have. They wouldn't have got me. I give one karate kick and they go flying. Then I take them like this, bang them like this and throw them like that. " Vasi pranced all around the kitchen demonstrating how he would have dealt with the hijackers. "Why you didn't fight, *Parti?*"

Parvathy didn't mind the boy but she could see that his mother was embarrassed. She scolded him, "That's enough now, Vasi. Go and play outside."

Instead Vasi ran up to Parvathy again. "I give them one kick like this and they dead." Sundari grabbed him, took him into the sitting room and set him in front of the TV to subdue him. She came back quite contrite. Parvathy wanted to tell her not to punish Vasi but Sundari didn't give her a chance. "Aunty, I'm so sorry. What an awful thing to happen! These days, you aren't safe anywhere. When I was putting Vasi in the car to come here, I saw some funny looking characters watching me. The way I jumped into the car, so fast, locked up and dashed off. How terrible Aunty! Where did it happen?"

Before Parvathy could open her mouth, Mulligay answered, "In Nelson Mandela Haven." Parvathy was annoyed especially when she saw them exchanging knowing looks. They had never been to the informal settlement, so what did they know? But they were going on like a couple of experts.

"What can you expect? That's a squatter camp! A dangerous place. Don't know why anyone wants to go there. We should keep out of those places. You went there alone?"

"She goes every Tuesday. Alone!" Mulligay nodded slowly and significantly. "They must have been watching her."

"Ya, you an easy target, Aunty. With all this grey hair. Ts, ts, ts," Sundari shook her head.

But Parvathy had stopped listening. She simply insisted, "Kogila is gone." In her mind's eye she could still see Kogila's grin. When Sundari raised her eyebrows questioningly at her mother, Parvathy became impatient.

Mulligay explained, "The car - Aunty Parvathy's car. She named her Kogila." She saw Sundari's eyes widen as she pressed her lips together to choke back laughter. Mulligay continued, "They took all her keys. Now she can't get into the house. I must call Morgan. He must bring a locksmith." When Mulligay went off to telephone her son, Sundari sat down but Parvathy didn't want to talk to her. She sat quietly until thoughts of Kogila overcame her again and words came tumbling out. "What am I going to do? My Kogila left me. We did everything together. Now I'm all alone. I don't know how I will manage. What use is my life now?"

"What can you do, Aunty? When your time comes you got to go. Your car is gone. You won't get it back. It's not your car anymore." A huge sob escaped Parvathy. How could this girl say something like that? What did she know about loss?

"Don't cry, Aunty." Parvathy wanted her to shut up but she went on and on. "You are a Hindu. You believe in reincarnation. You know Kogila will come back. Not to you, but she will come back. In another form." Parvathy couldn't believe what she was hearing. This girl had completely wiped her Kogila out of existence. Then Sundari floated off into her own fantasy. Sitting there, right in front of Parvathy, she was prattling on, "In another form, perhaps a Mercedes sports car." Parvathy saw the dreamy look in her eyes and turned her head away in annoyance. If only she could go home. Mulligay returned to assure her that Morgan was on his way and she would soon be in her own house.

"Have you had any lunch? I can dish up quickly."

"No, thank you very much. I can't eat anything."

"But it's three o' clock. You went out early this morning; you must be starving."

"Thank you, Mulligay. But I can't eat. How can I eat when Kogila is gone?" When she saw Sundari trying to hide her smile, she stood up and announced that she would wait in her own yard. But Mulligay forced her back into her chair and sent her daughter out of the kitchen.

Late that afternoon, Parvathy was back in her house. She wanted to lie down but Mulligay was right behind her. And before she knew it, Mulligay had taken charge of proceedings. She ignored Parvathy's protests and set Sundari the task of calling all the neighbours and friends. Then she reorganised Parvathy's sitting room. She pushed the chairs and the sofa against the walls, "For visitors who come to commiserate," she said. She propelled Parvathy into her bedroom, dressed her in a white sari and seated her in the living-room, next to the *kuthuvillaku* (standing lamp) that she had fetched from her house with other brass vessels. Parvathy heard her whispering to Sundari, who was busy on the 'phone, "She doesn't even have a lamp in her house." She lit the lamp and the cube of camphor on the brass tray, set out flowers, banana, betel leaf, betel nut and ashes and lit the incense sticks in the little brass vases. Then she arranged all these ritual items around a garlanded photograph of Kogila. Parvathy, who kept dozing off, was only vaguely aware of what was happening.

When visitors began streaming in after sunset, Mulligay shook her and she opened her eyes and stared blankly. Why were they taking off their shoes and talking in reverential whispers? She thought she was dreaming when she saw them rotating the tray before Kogila's picture, drawing stripes of ash on their foreheads and sitting down along the walls in attitudes of mourning. When new arrivals entered, there were muted, *"Vanakams"* as they raised their hands in solemn greeting to all those seated along the walls. After the little ritual before Kogila's picture, the men went directly to the chairs on their side of the room where they sat, eyes downcast, whispering when they felt the necessity to speak. The women embraced Parvathy who slumped in their arms heavy with sleep. Each woman that entered tried to engage her in a whispered dialogue but she didn't respond. She knew this was a dream, a very strange dream.

When the women began chanting bhajans and singing kirtans and all joined in, Parvathy's head jerked back and suddenly she was wide awake and astonished at what she saw. *What are these people doing in my house?* Sundari popped her head out of the kitchen and called in a couple of women to help bring in the tea. In between her fits of dozing, Parvathy had caught whiffs of frying *goolgoolas, bhajias and vadès,* all vegetarian fare, the kind of stuff her neighbours made for religious ceremonies. She felt trapped. These people had invaded her home but she didn't have the energy to chase them out. When she heard Mulligay whispering to the women that next week there would be a *yetoo,* the eighth day ceremony after a funeral, and that the women were expected to come and cook for the occasion, she roused herself from her stupor.

"*Yetoo?* What is that for?"

"It's a very important ceremony."

"But what is it for?"

"You mustn't ask such things. There is always a *yetoo* when someone dies."

Parvathy burst out, "Who died?"

Mulligay ignored her question. "I already told everyone. They will all be coming on Monday. My son has arranged for a priest to conduct the yegyim." Parvathy screamed, "I don't care; I don't want any of this," but only a few croaking sounds issued from her throat. Mulligay just shook her head. "Sometimes, *Athè,* I think you deserve what's happening to you. You don't believe in anything. You didn't even do the pumpkin ceremony to bless the car? No wonder you were hijacked."

"She didn't bless the car!" The visitors were shocked.

"Where she goes to the temple?" Mulligay continued contemptuously.

"No wonder she was hijacked."

Parvathy tried to speak but everyone ignored her crackling noises.

"She doesn't come to the temple, she doesn't even light the lamp or pray and she's always running round to the squatter camps."

Then Sundari and her helpers came in from the kitchen with trays of tea and snacks and set them down ready for the end of the ceremonial activities. This was the signal for the last few bhajans. And while the group was solemnly singing the most reverential hymns, Parvathy, mad with frustration, was trying to collect her strength. She made a great effort and suddenly she was standing. The singing died down and she heard her neighbour's shocked voice, "What are you doing? We are in the middle of *Pinaki Ilaathe Perinthurai Perumane.*"

"What does it mean?" she managed to croak back.

"It's a very holy song. We always sing it at funerals."

"My Kogila is not dead," she croaked and as she stumbled out she was aware of women slapping hands across gaping mouths and men shaking their heads. She escaped to her bedroom, locked herself in, fell on the bed and was soon snoring away.

The next morning, she found her house back to normal. All the ritual paraphernalia was gone and the furniture back in place. What resounded in her head this morning were her own words, "Kogila is not dead." That gave her new resolve. She was going to get her back. For the next week, she was embroiled in battle with the insurance company.

When she phoned to tell them that Kogila was gone, she encountered
the same funereal mentality of her neighbours. The insurance agents
also regarded Kogila as deceased and wanted Parvathy to put in for a
replacement vehicle. But Kogila was not dead. "I only called to inform
you that Kogila has been stolen. I am not making a claim. I thought you
had to be informed."

No matter how many times she told them she was not making
a claim, she got the same stock response: If she was not prepared to
make a claim, there was nothing they could do for her.

At the end of the week, she got a call from Sergeant Mahlangu
of the border police at Osshoek. Her car had been found. The thieves
had tried to take it through a roadblock but the police had been given
such a good description that they had identified it easily, even though
it had Swazi number plates. Parvathy would have to go to Swaziland to
identify the car and sign for its release. Parvathy was delighted. She ran
over to her neighbour whom she had forgiven for consigning Kogila to
the dead. "Mulli, Mulli, they found Kogila. They found my car." Then
she ran back home to inform the Nelson Mandela Haven Police Station
where she had made her statement. Mahlangu had told her that the police
there would bring her out to Osshoek. But their telephone wasn't working.
So she telephoned ten different police stations in surrounding areas and
eventually located the sergeant, who had taken her statement. He had
been reassigned to another police station. She knew he would be as glad
as she was that Kogila had been found.

She shouted into the 'phone, "They found Kogila. They found
her. She's on the Swazi border."

Parvathy knew that being a sergeant he couldn't display his
emotion and accepted the calmness in his tone when he asked, "Oh, Miss
Moonsami, did you get your wallet back?" Parvathy was puzzled. "They
found it the same day. It's at Nelson Mandela Police Station." Parvathy
was shocked. They'd had her wallet for over a week and hadn't made
any attempt to inform her. She had to get to Nelson Mandela Haven right
away.

Parvathy ran over to her neighbours again and Morgan took her
to the police station where she collected her wallet and asked when they
would take her to Osshoek. She found that they wouldn't commit
themselves to a time. Again Morgan helped her out. One of his clients
was going to Swaziland the next day and he made arrangements for her
to go with him. Parvathy called Inspector Mahlangu to tell him she was
coming and he insisted that she get a clearance letter from the insurance

company.

"But it's my car. You have a copy of my registration papers! "You must get the insurance company to fax me a clearance letter."

"It's my car."

"I need the letter from the Insurance Company."

So she called the insurance company again and was passed on from one to another of what seemed like a hundred different people and, while on hold in between, she learned the melody of Johan Strauss' *Voices of Spring*. Eventually, she found someone, The Sender-of-Faxes, who wouldn't help her because she had not made a claim.

"We need claim forms."

"I'm not claiming."

"We need claim forms."

"But it's my car."

For a couple of hours the calls went back and forth until The Sender-of-Faxes at last agreed to send off a fax stating that Parvathy had not made a claim but the police could release the vehicle to her.

The next day, she took the ride to Swaziland and was dropped off at Osshoek only to be told, "Inspector Mahlangu is not here. He went off early this morning." Parvathy collapsed in a chair. What was she to do now? She was stranded in a strange place. Her informant laughed, "Don't look so sad. I am Inspector Mahlangu. I just wanted to see what you would do?" Parvathy was not amused.

After the rituals of identification and filling out of forms, Parvathy eventually drove off with a much-chastened Kogila. Her gears were not working properly. The gear lock had been removed and had apparently thrown her second gear out of alignment. In the four-hour journey back, Parvathy's antennae were stretched to the limit as she struggled with the gears along strange roads. Through the mess of a windscreen that had been painted over for storage in the police lot and had not been cleaned properly, she probed the darkness for hijackers. She knew that Kogila too was tense and only concentrated on home. She had had her adventure and would be glad to return to normal. Parvathy was sure she was looking forward to a simple life again: resting in the garage and going to the store to pick up ginger jellies.

The Foreign Teacher

Peering through the window, they could see her, crouched in a corner, eyes rolling, two white vortexes in a pitch-black face with pigtails sticking out like little thorns around it.

"Eh, she looks mad. I told you she was a witch." Mrs. Chauke, the large woman who lived down the street, shuddered, "Lucky my Kulani didn't come for lessons today."

"Send for the inyanga," muttered Mr. Maswanganyi, another neighbour, "he will beat out the evil spirit."

"Au, she is a very good teacher. I don't think she's a witch." Mrs. Maluleke was delighted with Nyeleti's progress in Margaret's school. "Nyeleti likes her very much and look how good she speaks English. Just like Shangaan."

Mr. Maswanganyi who had not taken his eyes off the woman said, "Something's wrong. We must get her out. She might die." But the windows were shut tight and secured by burglar bars. Only a small fanlight was open. "That window up there ...but it's too small...."

"I'll call Nyeleti. She can climb through."

Mrs. Chauke became frantic. "Don't let her out! She'll kill us!" With a little scream, "Look, she's moving; coming near the window." Mrs. Chauke backed away from the window, out of the gate, and ploughed into the muddy road churned up by recent floods and covered with pools and dongas.

Mrs Maluleke ran to the fence, "Nyeleti, Nyeleti, come quickly. We must help your teacher."

Mrs. Chauke, ankle-deep in mud, turned in horror. "Are you mad? Are you going to send your daughter in there with a witch? What if she kills her?"

Nyeleti, who had been watching TV, came running out. Mr. Maswanganyi hoisted her up and her skinny little frame slithered through the fanlight. When she saw her teacher in the corner, Nyeleti got a fright but pulled herself together and approached cautiously. Meanwhile, her mother and Mr Maswanganyi were shouting to her to get away from the teacher and open the front door. But Nyeleti crept up behind Margaret, took something from her pocket and slipped it into her teacher's mouth. Within a few minutes, the woman came round. Her eyes focused normally and she stood up. She saw Nyeleti and smiled.

"Hullo, Nyeleti, what are you doing here? Did you come for a library book?" Then Margaret saw Mr. Maswanganyi and Mrs. Maluleke knocking wildly on the windows. She opened one. "Hullo, Sam. Hullo Martha. Why are you standing outside? Come in. Come in."

Mrs. Chauke struggling through the mud shouted out, "What's happening? What is she doing now? Is Nyeleti dead?"

Margaret called to her, "Hullo, Beauty. Does Kulani want a library book?"

Margaret Anan, a tiny woman from Ghana, had come to South Africa to teach English in a private school in Venda. After the contract expired, she was left to her own devices. Being very resourceful, she opened her own school to which the locals gave full support. But they were suspicious of her. She was foreign, very black, walked too fast, was all alone and had the magical ability of getting children to read and speak English fluently within a year.

When Mrs Chauke saw Margaret at the window, smiling and inviting her to come in, she swung away, staggered through the mud and huffed to the safety of her own house. Margaret shrugged and turned to Mrs. Maluleke and Mr. Maswanganyi, who had entered the room. They kept looking nervously from her to little Nyeleti. Mrs. Maluleke stared at her daughter. *What was this child? What muti had she given this woman?*

"Are you feeling all right now, teacher?" Nyeleti took Margaret's hand.

"I'm perfectly fine. Why do you ask?"

"You were in the corner, your eyes all white."

"What are you talking about? I was having a nap. Goodness, it's six o'clock. Have I been asleep that long?"

"Nyeleti came through the window. You didn't see that?" Mrs. Maluleke burst out. "She put something in your mouth and then you were all right."

Mr Maswanganyi turned to Nyeleti, "What did you put in her mouth?"

"A sweet."

"A sweet?" Mrs Maluleke and Mr Maswanganyi turned incredulous eyes on Nyeleti.

"When my ma'am feels sick, she eats sweets."

Then it dawned on Margaret. "Oh my, I must have had an attack." She picked Nyeleti up and gave her a big hug. *"You clever girl."* She turned to Mrs. Maluleke. Your daughter saved my life. I'm diabetic. When my blood sugar drops too low, I lose consciousness. I always carry sweets in my bag in case of an emergency."

Mr. Maswanganyi and Mrs. Maluleke just stared.

The locals never quite got over this event but they continued to support Margaret's school. In fact, she was overwhelmed by the demand. As long as her witchcraft enabled their children to speak English fluently, they accepted her magical powers. But they remained vigilant.

In My Mother's Footsteps

Meenatchie's sister-in-law, Ambigay, came rushing into the kitchen, bright eyes mixed with seeming concern and the desire to gloat.

"*Unni*, I don't know how to tell you this." Meenatchie saw the feeble attempt to control her eagerness. "Logan is seeing that Kamala. I saw them walking down to the river. They were holding hands." Meenatchie saw the other two sisters-in-law look up - Salatchie in excitement, Thamyandhi with genuine concern.

Meenatchie didn't respond. She went on rolling out the *pur* for the *samoosas* she was making. This was not the first time she had heard of this friendship. People had been gossiping for weeks, but she had simply dismissed the rumours. This was just their desire to bring her down. She knew that deep down people resented her because she had always had the courage to stand up for what she believed in.

"*Unni*, I saw them with my own eyes."

Knowing her sister-in-law was waiting for a response, she simply said, "Thank you, Ambigay."

This did not satisfy Ambigay and she persisted, "But what are you going to do?" Meenatchie's rolling pin continued its steady rhythm. "What if he wants to marry her? They say he's been going out with her for months now." Meenatchie patted another ball of dough onto her board but her sister-in-law persisted. "What are you going to do?"

Meenatchie picked up the boxes that were under the table. "Please help me pack the *samoosas* and *achar* sandwiches. Vadivel Annè will be here to pick them up just now." They supplied the family cafè with *samoosas* and *achar* sandwiches for the late afternoon rush when people taking the bus to Atteridgeville and Saulsville stopped in on their way home from work. Sulkily, Ambigay turned to the packing and that was the end of her enquiry for the afternoon.

At the dinner table that evening, Meenatchie watched her son closely. Logan was in a very gay mood as he told the story of how members of the Pretoria Tamil League had caught the thief who had been stealing from the temple. "Uncle Aru," Meenatchie flinched, "and Uncle Soobiah hid in the *gopuram* for three weeks waiting for the thief. But he didn't come so they gave up the watch. They thought the thieving was all over and they could live with the loss of lamps and small statues."

Meenatchie couldn't look at her son; he was positively glowing as he spoke. Didn't he realise what he was doing to her? And here was her brother-in-law encouraging him.

Deva, Thamyandhi's husband, munching on a chilli as usual, coaxed Logan on. "But I thought you said they caught the thief."

"I'm coming to that." Logan's voice was full of merriment and Meenatchi couldn't shut it out. "The next day - all the *murthis* disappeared. I mean, the most important statues, Muruga, Velli, Devayanai and Ganesha. All gone. Straight after they gave up the vigil. They were wild with anger."

Deva laughed. "I would be too if I sat there for three weeks in the cold night losing all my sleep."

"You know how devout Uncle Aru is. But he was so angry he even shouted at the shrine. 'Mariamman, you are the goddess of strength, give us the strength to catch the thief.'"

"They didn't take Mariamman?" Even Thamyandhi was encouraging Logan.

Drops of perspiration pouring down his forehead, Deva laughed again. "Mariamman is too powerful."

Logan laughed too. Meenatchie couldn't stand the sound of his joyfulness. "Uncle Aru was seething." She flinched again. *Uncle Aru, Uncle Aru. Since when had that man become his uncle?* "He couldn't believe how he had been fooled. He was going to give the thief the thrashing of his life when he caught him. That night, Uncle Aru - he can see the *gopuram* from his veranda - was staring up at it when he suddenly picked up his torch and a stick and without a word to anyone dashed off to the temple. Aunty Jean was surprised and sent Bala after him. When they got to the temple, they found the gate open and ran in. They saw a shadow on the other side of the shrine so they split up, circled the shrine and trapped the thief. Uncle Aru grabbed him and began bashing him mercilessly. Bala had to pull him off. Uncle Aru didn't even know who he was beating."

"Who was it?" Ambigay's inquisitiveness always irritated Meenatchie.

"Philemon."

"Philemon! The cleaner who used to work at the temple?"

Logan nodded.

Mopping his face with a big handkerchief, Deva shook his head. "That boy was so lazy, the League had to fire him."

Logan laughed, "Apparently, for the three weeks that Uncle Aru and Uncle Soobiah were sitting at the bottom of the *gopuram* waiting to catch him, Philemon was at the top watching them."

Meenatchie cut short the laughter that erupted. "And where did you hear this story?" She could see Logan going on the defensive.

"Oh, Bala was telling us about it."

"Oh, were you visiting his house?" Bala was Aru's son.

'No, Bala and I were playing billiards at the caffy." He stood up quickly. "Anyway, I have to go. Please excuse me. I'm going to the dance at the Dougall Hall. A band from Jo'burg is playing this weekend."

But she wasn't going to let him off. "Who are you taking to the dance?"

He didn't look at her. "Just going with Vasu and some of the guys from the football club. Excuse me. I have to run. I promised to meet them at eight." And before she could question him further, he was gone.

Meenatchie, aware of Ambigay's sidelong glances, picked up some dishes and went off to the kitchen. But Ambigay was close on her heels, whispering, *"Unni,* I think he's going to the dance with that Kamala." Meenatchie gave her a look that quickly sent her back to help the others clear the table. Meenatchie deposited her dishes in the sink and went off to her room. She wouldn't subject herself to sly looks and whispers behind her back. She would leave them to gossip to their hearts' content while they were washing the dishes. She had had to put with their surreptitious laughter and giggling for too long.

Then she remembered that she hadn't put out the mince for the next day's samoosas. She would have to go back to the kitchen. As she approached, she heard Ambigay laughing, "Did you see *Unni's* face? Like a stone. No smiling, frowning, nothing. But I think she's boiling inside."

She stopped. She didn't want to, but she listened.

"How would you like it if your son was going out with that girl? She could hear contempt mixed with gloating in Salatchie's voice. Salatchie resented her because she had made a name for herself in the community. "You think he's serious about Kamala?"

"He must be. They not hiding anymore. I saw them walking hand in hand today." Only Ambigay could be so gleeful.

"Nowadays children, they don't care about our customs." Thamyandhi was the only one who wasn't titillated by the scandal.

Meenatchie nearly gasped out loud at what she heard next. *"Unni* doesn't mind." Salatchie spoke in a mocking tone. "I mean, she was in the passive resistance. She believes in equal rights. Chi, if it was my Gopal, before I can do anything, his father will give him such a clout, he won't be able to speak. But Gopal knows his culture. Not like Logan."

Ambigay jumped in eagerly. "That's true. Logan doesn't know what nation he is. He makes friends with everybody. He got friends in Eersterus and Atteridgeville."

"It's all *Unni's* fault. She's always talking about equal rights and rushing off to all the marches," Salatchie was sneering. "Remember that time when the children were still small, she went and sat on the Whites Only bench outside OK Bazaars and they locked her up. We had to take care of the children for three months. So, why is she angry now?"

"Ya, why she goes marching around fighting the gov'ment? Is that the way for an Indian woman to behave, marching in the streets and going to visit people in the prisons? And then she expects her son to respect our traditions."

Meenatchie had heard enough. She marched into the kitchen and her look told them that she had heard.

"Can I make you some tea?" Salatchie offered feebly but Meenatchie ignored her.

"I just came to take the mince out of the freezer." She couldn't keep the anger out of her voice. After she put the mince in the fridge, she turned abruptly and left the kitchen.

*   *   *

At the Dougall Hall, Logan paced about impatiently. "She should have been here by now."

"Hey man, you know how girls are. They like to make you wait." Vasu, the handsome striker from the Pretorians Football Club, lounging in his chair, surveyed the hall. Lots of pretty girls were throwing inviting glances at him but he was in no hurry. Logan knew Vasu loved the adulation. He and Vasu were the football stars of the location and they had great rapport on the field. It was as though they were inside each other's heads. One knew when the other was going to make a run for it and he provided back up. They were the highest scorers in the club and they always tried to outdo each other.

Then Logan spotted Kamala, "Ah, there she is," and dashed off as Vasu stood up leisurely and made his way across the room to where all the girls were waiting in anticipation.

Logan grabbed Kamala's hand, whirled her onto the floor and they swept off together. "Man, you make me mad."

Kamala arched her brows, "Oh?"

"I've been going crazy. I thought you'd never come." He burrowed his head in her neck.

"So you missed me."

"All the time." He tried to kiss her but she turned away

"Not in front of all these people."

Logan swept her to a quiet corner. "I want to get married right away."

"What do you mean right away?"

"We can go to court on Monday and get registered."

Kamala pulled herself out of his arms. "That's how my father got married but that's not what he wants for his sons and daughters."

Logan took her into his arms again and held her so close, she began to blush. "I don't care what anyone else wants. I want you. I'm in hell when I'm not with you." Kamala just stood there, head against his chest, body pressed against his, not breathing.

"Hey, what are you two doing in this dark corner?" Vasu's amusement forced them apart.

Kamala's face was red more from the heat of the embrace than the intrusion. "What do you want here? Aren't there enough girls in the room for you?"

"But Logan's got the best."

"Hey, keep your eyes off my girl. And go away."

'Oh come on broe, you've got the most beautiful girl and the best dancer in the room. Give me a break. Can I have one dance with her?"

"No. Go away." Vasu laughed, found a partner hovering behind him and swung her out onto the floor.

Logan sat down and pulled Kamala beside him. "I'm serious. I want to get married."

"So do I. But we will have to do it according to custom. You know my dad."

"Does that mean the family must make the proposal?" She nodded. "Damn. It's going to take forever."

"I'm not worth the wait?"

Logan pulled her to him and gave her a deep kiss. "I can't wait. I'm going crazy."

Kamala stood up. "There's only one way. I love you but I'm not going to hurt my parents. They never complain and they don't show it but they have suffered and if I can make it up to them in some small way, I will."

"All right, I'll talk to my mum."

*　*　*

The next morning, after she had cooked the mince and filled the samoosas, Meenatchie went out to buy a chicken from Mr Chinsamy on Eighth Street. She was busy examining the fowls in the coop when Jean entered the yard. She didn't turn round and went on looking for a nice, fat hen.

But Jean greeted her, "Hullo, Meena. How are you?"

Why was this woman talking to her? She had never encouraged any kind of acquaintance. But the woman persisted.

"I didn't see you at the Varaluxmi prayers last week." Then Jean laughed, "I suppose you don't need anymore good fortune."

Meenatchie frowned. Was this woman trying to lecture her about her religion? Jean had started wearing saris but anyone could see she wasn't Indian. She was too white. Today, she was even wearing a red dot on her forehead. What cheek! She didn't have the right; she got married in court. Aru's family had never accepted her but she had insinuated herself into the community and was even involved in temple functions. A Christian woman involved in the temple!

When Jean reached into her blouse and proudly pulled out her *thali*, the marriage cord, she was flabbergasted. "Look, I am wearing a *thali* now."

"But you're a Christian!"

"Not anymore. Not after Father O'Neal told me I was living like a pagan and couldn't receive communion. Aru and I went to the temple last week and had a small private wedding ceremony. We did it for my daughter. Kamala has been nagging us for a long time to have a Tamil ceremony. She keeps saying, 'Mummy, your civil marriage is not good enough. If you and Daddy don't go to the temple and get married properly, you won't be able to stand as my parents at my wedding.'

Meenatchie swung around with such force that she swiped Jean across the shoulder with the hen she was holding by the feet and it began squawking and jerking its head up. "What are you trying to tell me? Don't think I will let my Logan marry into your family. We are high caste people." She thrust the fowl back at Chinsamy and stalked out of the yard.

She abandoned the rest of her shopping, turned at the corner and stormed up Grand Street. So things had got that far. They were talking of a wedding now. Despite their reputation for kindness and generosity, that Aru and Jean were a cunning pair. Some bad *karma* had brought them into her life. Why had Aru married Jean? Why couldn't he have kept her as a mistress in the Cape Location - like other men? Why did he have to bring her into their community? And all those years ago when she first came, the *poosari* at the temple had welcomed her openheartedly. And Thamyandhi, her well-meaning but simple-minded sister-in-law, had befriended her, had taken her in hand, explained what was happening, shown her how to conduct herself in the rituals and had brought her among the women to help with temple chores and preparations for temple festivals.

Then Thamyandhi had come to her very proudly and told her of Jean's progress, modestly refraining from mentioning her role as mentor. Thamyandhi was counting on her approval but she got the surprise of her life when Meenatchie turned on her. Meenatchie knew that Thamyandhi admired her and was trying to emulate her. But fighting against a despotic government was different from dissipating one's culture. She would never forget the look on Thamyandhi's face when she scolded her for teaching a Coloured woman about their holy rituals.

Thamyandhi had surprised her with her outburst, "But you

believe in equal rights."

"That doesn't mean giving up your culture and traditions."

"I'm not doing that. I'm teaching Jean. I'm spreading our culture."

"You are cheapening it. You bring these half-castes into it and you turn it into a half-caste culture."

Thamyandhi's eyes had widened in shock. She had said nothing more but ever since that time had become distant. She obviously couldn't see how much they would lose with these kinds of inter-marriages. Coloured women were given to drinking, going to dances and picking up men. So many Indian men had mistresses in the Cape location, on the other side of Bloed Street, that she could actually see her own customs and traditions losing ground.

As she opened the door and walked into the lounge, she was confronted by the images of her husband and herself in the photograph on the wall. She shuddered. She tried to shut out thoughts of her husband. But Sadha's face kept rearing up in her mind's eye. She went to the kitchen to fry the samoosas. If she kept busy, she could forget. But it was no use. She couldn't stop thinking of him. He had been one of those always hanging around at the Orient Dance Hall, mixing with Coloureds and coming home drunk in the early hours of Saturday morning. She never confronted him but he would yell at her. "Why you don't look at me? Why you don't say anything? You think you too bleddy good because you mix up with the politicians? You call yourself a wife? You just a cold fish." Then he would beat her. It was an open secret that he was having an affair with a Coloured girl, sister of the leader of the Mafia gang, but no one spoke of it around her and she denied it even to herself. But when Sadha beat up his mistress, the Mafia gang came after him, there was a fight and he was stabbed to death. What a relief when he died. She dared not admit that to anyone and steadfastly remained in denial of her pernicious marriage. Her husband's violent end, however, had confirmed her view that Coloureds had no culture. And it irked her to see Aru with Jean. Instead of making her his mistress, he had actually married her, had married out of his community, against fierce opposition from his family who, after thirty years, still didn't speak to him. She hated to admit it but they were a devoted couple and their children were refined and good-natured.

After she had fried the samoosas and packed them in boxes

ready to be taken to the cafè, she picked up her tray and went to clean spices outside in the yard. Soon she was enjoying the afternoon sun on her back and thoughts of Jean and Aru and the trap they had set for her son, evaporated from her mind. The little spice trade that she ran from home had always kept her independent and she had really appreciated it in the days when she had been tied to an abusive husband. She should never have married; her only real joy had been her involvement in the political struggle. But in recent years with all the leaders in jail or out of the country, mass action had died down and people were working underground. And she was confined to the house.

Her mind drifted back to her childhood and to her parents. They had been just such a loving couple as Jean and Aru. Her mother had walked side by side with her father in everything he undertook. She had been in that first group of women resisters trying to get legal recognition for Indian marriages. Her mother had always laughed when she told stories of how they had battled to get arrested because the police hadn't known what to do with the dozen or so women walking around, hawking without licences. But her experiences in prison had been ghastly. They had been so cold and the food had been awful. When they left the prison after three months, they were practically skeletons and one had died soon after being released.

Meenatchie had always wanted to be like her mother. When her parents arranged a marriage for her, she looked forward to the same kind of happiness that her parents shared. She was ready to march alongside her husband in the liberation struggle. It had never occurred to her that her family's courage and activism were unusual; she had simply taken them for granted. She was shocked when she found that her husband shunned politics and expected her to stay home and be a good housewife.

But she couldn't do that. She defied her husband and found opportunities to be active. She went to jail during the Passive Resistance, to the very same prison in which her mother had been incarcerated. That had given her such strength that when the Defiance Campaign began, she was one of the first to volunteer. Marching alongside people asserting their right to freedom, she had felt truly alive. It was only in this house that she was a prisoner.

She was startled out of her reminiscences when Logan pulled up a mat and sat on the concrete paving next to her. *"Umma,* I have something very important to ask you."* Meenatchie's heart hardened.

Without looking up, she continued to sift through the cumin seeds. "I want to get married."

Meenatchie frowned. "You're too young, Logan. You must wait a few years."

"Ma, I'm twenty-five. I'm old enough. And there is this girl. I love her very much and I want to get married."

"So, you want to choose your wife. That's not your job. That is what I am supposed to do. Me and your uncles."

"But, Ma, it's different nowadays."

"Maybe in some low-caste families. But that's not how we do it."

"Please, *Umma*. You will like the girl I have chosen. She speaks Tamil better than I do and she reads and writes Tamil fluently. She goes to temple and her family fasts on the same days that we do. Her mother has the same *murthis* as you, in her home shrine - Vishnu, Shiva and Brahman."

"And who is this wonderful girl?"

Logan ignored the sarcasm and looked straight at her, "Uncle Aru's daughter, Kamala."

Meenatchie made a sudden motion to stand up and her tray went flying into the yard, scattering cumin seeds all around. The hens and chicks that were scratching in the sand came scuttling onto the concrete and began pecking and clucking in excitement. Meenatchie towered above her son who was on his knees trying to retrieve the cumin. "You want to marry into that family. You must be mad." She stormed off into the house. Logan jumped up and ran after her.

"*Umma*, wait, wait. Talk to me. *Umma*, what's wrong with her family?" Meenatchie bolted into her bedroom and slammed the door. Logan knocked and called, "Please, *Umma*, let's talk about this," but she just sat on her bed seething with rage. Then she heard a door in the passage open and Thamyandhi's voice asking, "What's the matter? What's going on?"

Logan shouted back. She knew he wanted her to hear him. "*Umma* is angry because I want to marry Kamala. I don't understand. What's her objection?"

Thamyandhi, trying to soothe him, spoke softly. Meenatchie, who could just catch her words, clenched her fists. "Give her time. Let her get used to the idea. I am sure she will come round."

"You think so, *Athè?* I don't believe it." He raised his voice even louder. "My mother! Of all people, my mother! She's just a hypocrite."

She heard Thamyandhi gasp. "Ah! Don't talk like that. You're angry now. You will regret what you say."

Then he began to bang on her door again and afraid he would force his way in, she jumped up and cringed in a corner. "Come out, Ma, I want to talk to you. Don't be a coward." He banged again. Then there was a commotion in the passage and she could hear Salatchie and Ambigay trying to calm him down. Their voices were muffled and she couldn't make out what was going on. Suddenly he was shouting at her through the door again. "I'm going to Uncle Aru's house and I'm going to ask him if I can marry Kamala." She heard him plunge out and the front door slam. There was a moment's silence and after that whispering, which receded up the passage and then died out.

Coward! Hypocrite! How could her own son call her such names? Coward? She who had faced police batons and police dogs? Just because she didn't want to talk to him when he was being so unreasonable? Flouting their traditions and going his own way, like a bastard who hadn't been brought up properly? What did he mean? Coward? Hypocrite? She couldn't get the words out of her mind.

*   *   *

Logan, angry and frustrated, walked quickly down the road. *I don't understand Umma's attitude. She won't even talk to me. She is being totally unreasonable. And Uncle Aru expects her to come with my uncles to bring a proposal. He is just as bad. Why is he so strict about customs? After all he married a Coloured woman. What am I going to do? My mother and Kamala's father! Between them, they'll drive me crazy. There's only one way. Kamala has to understand that. We have to get registered. We can't have an Indian wedding.* As he strode up to Uncle Aru's house, Bala, Kamala's brother, came out of the door.

"Hi Logan. If you've come to see Kamala, she's not here. She's gone with mother to see granny in Eersterus. Granny's not feeling too well and Mum has prepared some home remedies for her."

"I think I'll hang out at the caffy."

"Good idea. I'll come too. A game of billiards will do me some good."

As they set off, Bala noticed Logan's hangdog expression. "Anything wrong?"

"I just had a bust up with my mother."

"Oh, oh. I wondered when that was going to happen."

"What do you mean?"

"You know. Your Mum doesn't approve of my Mum."

"That's nonsense. My mother is just reserved that's all."

"Your Mum ignores my Mum altogether. She always avoids her. At the temple she keeps far from her."

"That's not true."

"Oh yes, it is. Kamala and I always do our best to protect Mum. My Dad is so proud of the way Mum has adapted to Tamil customs that he only sees her outshining all the other women. He doesn't see some of them sniggering."

Logan was silent. He had heard his aunts, Salatchie and Ambigay, making fun of Aunty Jean. He put it down to their narrow-mindedness. He had never heard his mother or aunt Thamyandhi mocking Aunty Jean. Bala was probably bitter because Parvathy, one of Kamala's friends, had rejected him despite the fact that he had his mother's white skin and golden brown hair.

When they arrived at the cafè, they found Vasu sitting at one of the little tables. The usual teasing light was missing from his downcast eyes and his mouth was pulled into a kind of snarl.

"Hey, what's up, Vasu. Man look at you. I don't know if I should hang around you guys today. You both look like murder." Bala grinned and went off to get cokes from Uncle Deva who was on duty.

"What's bothering you, Vasu?"

"I don't know what I'm going to do?" Vasu was sullen. "I'm in a fucking bind." Logan waited for him to continue. Bala came back, set the cokes down, pushed the back of the chair to the table, swung his leg over the seat and settled down.

Taking one look at his friends, he shook his head. "If you two are holding a wake, I think I'll go and get some action at the billiard table."

Vasu pulled his tall frame up. "Yeah, let's play. I need distraction,."
And they went over to the table. The cafè was not too busy so Uncle
Deva sat down with Logan.

"The Club not meeting today?"

"No *Sinuppa*, we're not playing tomorrow."

"When's your next game?"

"Next Sunday. We're playing Cambridge."

"I suppose it's going to be a dirty fight with those bastards."

"We've got our own strongmen. We can handle it."

"No, don't tell me that. I can't forget how the gang followed
you home and tried to beat you up. If me and Soma and Vadivel didn't
come out and chase them off, I doubt you'd still be playing soccer." He
turned his gaze to Vasu and Bala. "What's the matter with Vasu? He's
been sitting here for an hour now with his face all pulled up." He looked
at his nephew. "You too. Why you look so sour?"

"It's *Umma*. I told her I want to marry Kamala and she just blew
up. What should I do, *Sinuppa?* Can you talk to her for me?"

"Why you want to get mixed up with Kamala? You know you
asking for trouble."

"I don't believe this. I always thought our family was different.
I can understand any other family objecting. But our family? *Thatha*
started the resistance movement. *Umma* and *Uppa* went to jail. You went
to jail. So what was that all about? Just pretence? "

"Now, now, don't get so worked up. I like Kamala. If you want
to marry her, that's fine with me."

"Will you speak to *Umma?*"

A customer walked in and Uncle Deva stood up. "I'll see what
I can do."

Logan strolled over to the billiard table.

Bala was jubilant. "That's it. Game over. I win. Hey Logan, can
you believe it? I beat Vasu. He's off form today. Completely off form.
Lucky we aren't playing any matches this weekend."

Vasu pulled on his jacket. "I'm going for a walk." He strode off
with Logan and Bala running to keep up with him. When they got to the
river, they sat under a tree. "What am I gonna do, guys? Patsy's pregnant."
Patsy was Vasu's favourite dance partner but Logan and Bala had no
idea that they were seeing each other. Vasu always gave the impression

that he was playing the field. "What am I going to do? What the hell am I going to do?"

Bala was up and standing over Vasu, his eyes flashing with anger. "Fuck you, man. You're talking about my cousin." Vasu just sat there dejected. "You better say you're going to marry her."

"I don't want to get married." Bala was about to jump on him but Logan held him back.

Struggling to free himself, Bala shouted, "You bastard. You treat her like a whore just because she's Coloured."

"That's got nothing to do with it. I just don't want to get married. I'm not ready for it."

"So what the hell you make her pregnant for?"

"Cool down, Bala. This could happen to any of us."

"Stick up for him, that's right. All you bloody char ous stick together. I'm getting out of here." Bala pulled himself out of Logan's grip and went rushing off along the riverbank.

Logan sat down beside Vasu. "Do you love her?"

"I suppose so. I have never given marriage a thought. I don't want this responsibility."

"Have you talked to Patsy about all this?"

"She just wants to get married. She is so afraid I am going to do what other Indian guys do. Dump her or keep her as a mistress in Eersterus. I can't talk to my parents. They'll kill me. What am I going to do? What would you do?"

Logan put his arm around his friend. "I wish I knew. If you loved her, it would be easy."

When darkness began to set in, they walked back; Vasu went home to Jerusalem Street and Logan to the end of Eighth Street to Aru Mamè's house.

Aru and Jean were on the sofa in the sitting room. Aru was reading a passage from the *Thirukurral* and explaining its meaning. When they had married, twenty six years before, Jean had committed herself to learning everything she could about her husband's culture. Ever since then, even though she was a Methodist, she had studied Tamil scriptures with him and had come to understand Hindu rituals and customs better than most people in the location. Although she did not speak Tamil, she understood it well and was very proud of her children, the most outstanding Tamil scholars in the community.

When Logan walked in, they stopped their study to welcome him. "Kamala is in the kitchen."

"No, Uncle Aru, Aunty Jean, I want to talk to you." Aru and Jean exchanged glances. Logan was struggling, not knowing how to broach the subject.

Jean decided to help him out. "Is it about Kamala?"

"Yes. Thank you, aunty. Uncle, I know you don't want to hear this from me. I know you want my mother and my *sinuppas* to come and speak to you. I know this is a family to family matter but...I don't know how to say this...

Again Jean came to his rescue. "Your family doesn't support you."

"Yes, thank you, aunty. I want to marry Kamala but my mother won't hear of it. I don't know if my *sinuppas* will support me. So I have come to speak for myself. Please forgive me. But I love her very much."

Aru looked him straight in the eye. "You know marriage is meant to bring two families together, not just the boy and the girl. There is no such thing as a love match in our tradition."

Jean put her hand on her husband's arm. "Love is a new tradition. Maybe we are the ones who started it."

Aru smiled. "You know, they say history repeats itself. I'm looking at you and I see myself twenty-six years ago. I brought my children up very strictly in the Tamil culture. That way, I thought things would be fine for them. But here it is again."

"I don't understand it! You kept out of politics. You never joined the marches or went to prison. And you are such a traditionalist when it comes to Tamil customs - But you married Aunty Jean!"

Jean laughed. "This arch traditionalist broke all the rules and customs when he got married."

"Uncle, I am going to speak to my *sinuppas* and see if they will support me. If they don't, will you allow me to make the proposal myself?"

Jean looked archly at her husband. "Oh you'd better. Who knows what will happen if you don't. He and Kamala could run off to the court and get registered."

Aru's eyes were twinkling as he looked at Jean and their wedding flashed before him. They had had to go to court twice. The first time, the magistrate refused to marry them because he thought Jean was white. The second time, he was at court, with no wedding ring and no understanding of how marriages based on Christian customs are conducted.

"No, no," he said mildly, "we don't want to make that the custom in this family. I am sure we can work it out."

Jean laughed, "Why don't you go in the kitchen and ask Kamala to make you some tea."

As Logan moved off to the kitchen to find Kamala, he heard Aru as he closed the *Thirukurral* and turned loving eyes on Jean. "It seems love is stronger than tradition. Without your love, my tradition is nothing."

*   *   *

That night Meenatchie waited on the veranda for Logan to come home. It was nearly midnight when she saw him wearily trudging along the pavement. As he came up the steps, he saw her sitting in the dark and stopped.

"What are you doing out here so late?"

"I was waiting for you."

"Why? Have you changed your mind?"

"No. I want to talk to you."

"We have nothing to talk about. Uncle Aru has accepted my proposal and I am going to get married."

"Please. Sit here and let me explain why you should not be doing this."

"You're too late..."

"Now who is the coward?"

He hesitated for a moment and then slouched down in the wicker chair next to her. "I'll listen, but nothing you can say will change my mind."

"Don't you understand what you are doing? You are destroying your own culture. People who lose their culture, lose their way? They become imitations and pick up the most superficial and worst aspects of other cultures. They are like watered down vinegar, weak and flat."

"*Umma*, why are you always demonstrating against the

government?"

She couldn't understand this sudden digression. "What's that got to do with this?"

"Everything. You sound just like the government."

"What! I sound like the government?"

"You've swallowed whole their theory of separate development. This culture that you keep talking about doesn't stay fixed, *Umma*. Our forefathers who came from India were very different from us. They spoke a different language, they wore different clothes and they had different life experiences. Marrying Kamala is not going to make me lose my way. I have already taken a different path and Kamala, just like you, will try to bring me back to the old ways. Uncle Aru is very traditional and his children follow the old customs even more strictly than you do."

"How can they? They are half-castes."

She expected him to explode; instead he turned a weary smile on her. "There you go again; sounding just like the government. Wake up, Ma, we are all half-castes." He got up and was about to go in but he bent down first and kissed her on the forehead. "Thank you. You are the one who put me on a new road. Good night, Ma." He grinned, "Don't picket my wedding."

After he had gone in, she stayed out there in the dark, stunned. Who was this boy, no, this man, who had just accused her of being a racist? Accused her of siding with a government she hated and had fought against? He didn't understand. She had nothing against other races as long as . . . she stopped herself. She couldn't finish the thought and her cheeks became hot. Oh God, what had her life been about?

What had she been struggling against? She went over and over and over the marches, the imprisonments, the protests, trying to find the central belief that had driven her but all she could see was her mother's determination, her mother's commitment, her mother's sacrifice. Where were her own? She found herself negotiating a minefield of rationalisations as she tried to find what she had committed herself to. What was it? A tradition? Not a conviction? Nothing was clear anymore.

As the first rays of the sun began to streak the sky, she involuntarily spoke out loud, "How could *I* have put him on a new road?"

She didn't understand. Even more incomprehensible - what was this strange, powerful feeling of pride that was beginning to emanate from the core of her being as she thought of her son?

Misfit

"Before Mom died, she became a Christian.'

They were all at dinner at Radha's home and Pushpa absorbed the shock without making it apparent. "Was that before I came out to see her?"

"Four, maybe five weeks before she died. I talked to her and then the minister from our church went to see her and she accepted Jesus as her saviour." Radha passed her the mashed potatoes. Pushpa said nothing.

Pushpa was here for Leela's wedding. She had last visited some ten years before, just a few weeks preceding her sister's death. She had heard nothing of the conversion then, not even from her sister. And she couldn't believe it. At the time, Luxmi, who had had a tumour removed from her brain, was reliving her childhood in the Asiatic Bazaar in Pretoria and making little connection with the present. Why would she convert? She and her husband, Ashok, had lived lives free of religious dogma. Why would she change? Was it because she knew she was dying? It couldn't be.

Pushpa thought back to the weeks she had spent with Luxmi before her death. Her sister had been eager to share with her videos of the musicals starring Jeanette MacDonald and Nelson Eddy that they had loved as children. But Luxmi hadn't had the energy to watch for more than a few minutes. And though she was often disorientated - there were times when she mistook Pushpa for Radha - she was always aware of her impending death, but had never once referred to any conversion.

A year or two after her death, Ashok married again - into a Christian family. On the day of her arrival from South Africa, Pushpa learned that Ashok's wife, Dora, was seriously ill in hospital. Subash, who had fetched her from the airport, told her that his father wanted her to meet Dora, if she didn't mind. So she went to the hospital with Subash, his wife, Mandy, and the children. They found Ashok seated at the bedside of a very frail looking woman with tubes in her nose and a catheter hanging at the side. Subash and Mandy greeted Dora with loving compassion. Pushpa shook hands with her and murmured a wish for her quick recovery.

"I was so looking forward to the wedding," Dora informed her, tears glistening in her blue eyes. "Leela is such a beautiful girl. She is like a daughter to me and now I am going to miss her wedding." Ashok leaned forward, took her hand and squeezed it to comfort her and share her pain. Pushpa felt like an intruder in this intimate family circle. She stood outside herself watching herself watching instead of participating. But being on the outside came naturally to her. Having lived alone for so long, more than half her life, she had lost the capacity for intimate relationships and demonstrations of affection.

So what was she doing here in the midst of a wedding celebration, especially when she regarded all rituals and rites as superstition? Leela had wanted her there, to stand in for her mother at the ceremony. Pushpa, thoughtlessly, had agreed. She had believed that she could do it. Thirty years before, she had been part of the family, had helped to bring up her sister's children and had been the indulgent aunt who adored and spoilt her nieces and nephew. But they were grown-ups now, not the little kids she used to kiss and cuddle, and they were strangers. It was only when she got to the States that she fully realised that she was completely unqualified to be her sister's surrogate.

When Subash took her to Ashok's home the day before the wedding, they found Leela waiting for them. Ashok was at the hospital. Pushpa was to help Subash baby-sit while Mandy went off with Leela and Radha to decorate the church. As soon as the children realised that their mother was leaving them, they began a loud tearful protest. Pushpa tried to comfort them, but the children looked quite through this stranger trying to insinuate herself into the family. Little Joshua eventually allowed her to hold him but three year old, Deborah, saw her as an outsider and would have nothing to do with her. Fortunately, Subash, who was wonderful with his children, gentle and attentive, saved the day and they were soon playing together happily.

When Ashok, who had spent the whole morning at the hospital, came back, Pushpa sat down to chat with him and silently registered the Bible in his hand. She enquired after Dora and commiserated with him on having to minister to yet another patient. Her sister, Luxmi, had been completely helpless after the brain surgery and Ashok had had to tend her like a baby. Now here was Dora, fairly helpless but fortunately, in good mental health. While they were talking, Pushpa, who had been priding herself on being totally civilized and behaving quite like a human, suddenly found herself on the verge of losing her temper.

"When you go back to South Africa, you must tell Vishnu about Luxmi's death." Pushpa stared; she could feel that her look was hostile. Luxmi had died ten years before. What was this sudden need on Ashok's part to send a message to Vishnu?

" I live in a different province. I never see Vishnu. I haven't seen him for thirty years. I have no idea where he is."

"Yes, but he should know." Pushpa said nothing. She was trying to get beyond her annoyance in order to understand her brother-in-law's need to communicate with a man he had never met; a man who had been his wife's lover over thirty years before. Charming, handsome Vishnu was a married man and Luxmi had been the other woman. He had kept her on a string, making the usual promises of leaving his wife and children, and when Luxmi finally admitted that she was just being used, she applied for a teaching post in England and left the country. In London, she met Ashok, a student from Bombay, married him and went to live in India. When their first child, Radha, was two years old, they emigrated to the States. That was over thirty years ago. So why dredge up the question of Vishnu now? Pushpa didn't even know if he was still alive.

Pushpa thought it must be her fault. Perhaps Ashok was uncomfortable with her because he could feel that she was merely an observer and had translated her detachment as disapproval. Besides, he had not informed her when he married Dora. So perhaps he was feeling guilty about that and had brought up the ghost of Vishnu to even the balance. Because Pushpa was not demonstrative, he couldn't see that she really was very happy that he had married again. If he had converted and that made him happy, she was glad. Dora's people had taken Ashok to their bosoms and he had more than a wife now, he had an extended family and a very caring one from what she could see. Ashok was charming and personable but she had always regarded him as selfish and felt he could have been a better husband to Luxmi. She could see that he was a better husband to Dora. Was it because he was now a Christian? Perhaps his concern for Vishnu was also Christian compassion.

That evening, they went to the wedding rehearsal at the church. Leela was in charge of operations and Pushpa, who had very little experience of Christian weddings, of any wedding ceremonies actually, was surprised to see how much the whole responsibility fell upon the bride. She was impressed as she watched Leela giving instructions to all the bridesmaids, her fiancè, Alan, his attendants, the parents, the flower girls and ring bearer, and even to Subash, an ordained minister, who would be performing the ceremony. Pushpa, standing in for Luxmi, was to light the mother's candle for the bride. It was a coordinated activity that she had to perform with Elizabeth, Alan's mother, who would be lighting a candle for her son. After all the participants had walked through their functions and understood where they were to be seated, they all went off to a reception. Pushpa wondered why they had to rehearse the reception.

The next day, the day of the wedding, a couple of things that everyone else took for granted surprised Pushpa. She was not aware that family members were escorted individually down the aisle to their seats. When her turn came, she took the arm of a very obliging usher and, smiling regally to hide her embarrassment, walked with him to her seat. She hated being on display. What a poor substitute for her sister! Here she was, conscious of her own embarrassment, when she should be thinking of Leela. Then came the moment to light the mothers' candles and she and Elizabeth stood up together as they had practised. Elizabeth was very nervous. As they took hold of the taper, she looked Pushpa squarely in the eye and said, "We can do this." Pushpa immediately realised that unlike Elizabeth, she was empty of the kind of feeling and connectedness that a mother would have at such a time. Hers was simply a mechanical performance.

The bridesmaids and groomsmen entered next, followed by a stunning trio: the ring bearer, Radha's six-year old, Timothy, and the two flower girls, Radha's four-year old, Sylvia, and Subash and Mandy's little Deborah. After Deborah had duly emptied her tiny basket of rose petals, she looked about a little confused and was about to return the way she had come in when Geoffrey, Radha's husband, rushed forward and brought her to her seat. Pushpa wanted to hug and kiss the children as she used to hug and kiss Radha, Subash and Leela, but she couldn't. Ashok then entered with Leela on his arm; she was an exceptionally beautiful bride and as she met her groom at the altar steps, the ritual turned into an oratorio. Leela, a musician, had interspersed the ceremony with musical interludes performed by a choir, soloists, and a duo. Pushpa, observing everything, wished she could shake off her objectivity and become involved. She knew she was letting Luxmi down very badly.

In the middle of proceedings, Leela and Alan suddenly left the altar and went to honour their parents. Pushpa was taken aback to find Leela in front of her holding out a rose. Then Leela went to embrace her father. Pushpa bit her lip; she should have hugged her niece. When the bride and groom returned to their places, the ceremony continued with Subash adding light-hearted comments about being the bride's brother and reminding Alan that Big Brother was watching. Luxmi was probably watching her sister!

After the wedding, the couple together with their parents took their places in the foyer to receive the congratulations of the guests. Pushpa pulled out her camera, an attempt to become involved. She was a notoriously bad photographer and joked that she would have been useful in the French Revolution because she was very good at beheading people. But still she went clicking away, capturing one headless person after another. She did not go to the reception that evening. At the previous night's dinner, she had sat silent and alone at a table full of strangers. She couldn't do it again. Luxmi was probably shaking her head.

The next day, they all spent the afternoon at the 'opening of presents' party at Alan's parents' home. Pushpa's present had been an incredibly inappropriate one. She had brought a statue of Sarasvathi, Goddess of Music and Education, and hadn't for one moment thought of the impact that would have in a Christian environment. For her, the statue was simply a connection with music, Leela's field, and a decorative object. Leela had opened the present the day before the wedding at Ashok's home and the family's polite enthusiasm had suddenly made Pushpa see it as a pagan object; not that she had anything against paganism - that was just religion at a different level. Her present did not surface with the others.

After the party, they left for Radha's place. And it was at dinner that Radha made the startling announcement, startling only to Pushpa, that Luxmi had converted before she died. Pushpa accepted Ashok's conversion but she could not accept Luxmi's. Later, when Pushpa asked Subash about it, he was reticent. Perhaps he was embarrassed because he knew his aunt was not a believer. All he said was, "Radha belongs to a different church. In my church, we don't believe in proselytising. I don't know exactly what happened. But it seems Mom agreed to accept Christ."

Sensing her nephew's discomfort, Pushpa did not pursue the topic. But she continued her enquiry in her head. Why hadn't Luxmi mentioned it to her? Had she suddenly become superstitious because she was dying? At the time, Pushpa had thought she had entered into her sister's interior world but now she realised that all she had seen had been the external suffering - a woman enduring the humiliation of an illness that had reduced her to total dependence and robbed her of her dignity. Pushpa had loved her sister more than anyone in the world, but could it be that she had never really known her?

It was a devastating realisation. Had she been as perfunctory a sister as she had been a mother at the wedding? A mysterious and tortured soul had lurked behind Luxmi's remote look and Pushpa had not seen it. Radha must have and had responded to it as a daughter and a devout Christian. Suddenly, the image of her niece as the little child she had helped to bring up, disintegrated. Radha now stood as an independent person, a woman with values and commitments totally divergent from her own. Had she known her mother better than Pushpa knew her sister?

Pushpa fought the idea. Luxmi had spent her life suppressing her own interests and needs in order to become the quintessential mother. Privately, Pushpa had deplored this. When Luxmi was dying and Radha asked her to become a Christian, it was possible that she had been in no condition to understand what was going on. If, however, she had understood and acquiesced to her daughter's request, Pushpa felt quite certain it was in pursuit of her role as mother supreme. Luxmi had always done what she felt was best for her children. She had never imposed her own beliefs or discouraged them from pursuing their own. She had done everything for their happiness. Or so she had thought. Coming from apartheid South Africa, a racially segregated society, she had not experienced xenophobia and racism at the social level, that is, within the racial ghetto where people were all of the same background.

But her children, living in a mixed society, had been subjected to prejudice from the time they were toddlers. They had spent their childhood years unconsciously fighting for a place in the mainstream. Involuntarily, they had known that they did not want to be part of a despised minority culture and had adopted mainstream values and beliefs. They had become Christians. When she had first heard of their conversions, Pushpa had accepted with her usual objectivity - objectivity, she realised now, that covered condescension.

She looked down on all attempts to bring the glorious mystery of the creation under human control, to name it, totemise it and project anthropomorphism on it. These were reactions of fear, not a willingness to embrace the wonder of it all. She loved that it was a mystery, that it had inspired awesome human efforts and that it would always withstand religion's attempts to contain it. She regarded religion as a pragmatic means to keep people civilized and was proud that she did not need external inducements to be a decent human being because she understood that it was essential to be one. But had her beliefs made her a decent human being? Had she not looked down on those with different views and withdrawn into herself? In addition to being a pseudo sister and mother, was she also a pseudo aunt who had not understood her nieces' and nephew's needs?

For the first time, she was being made to recognise fully, her nieces' and nephew's angst. They had struggled against prejudice all their lives and didn't need her intolerance as well. As she looked at them now, she was filled with gratitude and admiration. They could have been driven in destructive directions. But they had found the church. Religion had provided them with answers to real emotional and psychological needs. And when Luxmi was dying, Radha had ministered to her mother's pain in the same way as she had ministered to her own. Pushpa knew that Luxmi had never undertaken a spiritual quest. Her religion had been motherhood and she had remained its devotee until the very end. If she had become a Christian, it had been for her daughter. Not for herself. Her conversion had been complete acceptance of her child as an individual. Luxmi had known how to be a decent human being.

Before dropping Pushpa off at the airport the next day, Radha, Subash and their families took her to the hospital to say goodbye to Dora. They found Ashok steadfastly at his wife's bedside. Pushpa watched the children embracing Dora with filial affection and Dora responding to them as a mother and grandmother. They were all devout Christians together. And Pushpa saw that she hadn't been required to take Luxmi's place. Dora had more than filled that gap and should have been the one to light the mother's candle for Leela.

Holding hands, Ashok and his family formed a circle around the bed and Radha prayed for Dora. Pushpa watched from outside the circle as Radha asked Jesus to heal and bless Dora. After the prayer, as the group was leaving, Pushpa went up to Dora to say goodbye and wish her better health. "Leela gave me this rose during the wedding service. It is meant for her mother. You are more her mother than I could ever be. This is for you."

A Dying Wish

"Om namasivaya, om namasivaya," the dirge floated like a ghost around the room, gathering substance from the vaporous fumes issuing from the burning incense in the clay lamp, the camphor on the little round brass tray and the incense sticks in brass holders. The women in their dark silk saris, singing and keeping time to the beat of the cymbals, eyes trance-like in sanctimonious rapture, droned on and on. Like a circle of vultures, they sat around the bed, their sombre religious fervour suffocating the woman who lay before them, eyes wide with despair. When she began coughing, their fervour grew apace. They began to push for the end and the mournful singing took on a frantic momentum. But instead of giving up the ghost, she got out of bed, walked to the window, pulled back the curtains, threw open the windows and, in her nightie, stood with her back to them breathing in the fresh air. She had broken the spell.

The women stared, nonplussed. Perhaps she was too ill to realize that all this was for her own good. Here they were, women with families, sacrificing their time to unite her to Brahman, the universal soul. But what did this woman know? They shook their heads in disapproval and muttering in Tamil about "Bushmen" and uncultured people, slowly began to disperse. They would come back later. It was their duty. After all she was part of their family by virtue of her marriage to Perumal and they owed it to him. They would do it, no matter how unappreciated their sacrifice and concern.

* * *

As they were leaving Pat, the dying woman's sister, entered the room. Her powerful eyes took in the spectacle and disapproval could be read in every glance and turn of her head. The women filed out past her. Some shook her hand and made consoling noises. One woman, Devaki, who had stood throughout the whole procedure, indicating her rejection of it, was the last to come forward.

She whispered to the sister standing in the doorway. "This is wrong. It is very cruel. These people are singing songs for the dead."

Pat put her arm around Devaki's shoulders. "Dolores doesn't understand the songs." But Pat could see she was not convinced. After all, Dolores had been part of this community for nearly twenty years. Devaki turned to look at the skinny figure standing at the window and her eyes filled with tears. She slipped out of the room before she could lose control. Pat went up to Dolores and put strong, comforting arms around her and gently guided her back into bed.

"I'm so glad to see you. " Dolores could hardly speak. "Have you spoken to Father Raymond? Will he come to baptize me?"

Pat looked sadly at her sister. "He will come to see you, but he won't baptize you. Your husband and in-laws won't allow it."

Dolores looked distraught. "Daddy would have allowed it, wouldn't he? I mean, now that I am dying."

Their father, a Hindu man, had not allowed them to be baptized even though they had earnestly begged him when they were still teenagers. Their mother had been a devout Catholic but when she married out of the church, she was excommunicated. Their father had not wanted them to suffer as she had done. Like Mahatma Gandhi, he revered all religions and would have had no objections to his daughters becoming Catholics. In fact, they had attended church regularly with their mother. But they had all seen her pain at not being able to receive the Eucharist. He did not want to expose his daughters to the same kind of pain, especially as excommunication made no sense to him.

Pat turned to her sister. "Yes, Daddy would have allowed it."

Dolores smiled. "When is Father Raymond coming to see me? Perhaps, he can do it without them seeing." Pat didn't know what to say. "Just sit by me. I want to take a small nap before Peru gets home for dinner. You must be here when I wake up," she struggled to whisper. Perumal, Dolores's husband, was a traditional Tamil man and she had always put his needs first. Even now, ill as she was, she wanted to be there, ready to serve his dinner, as he would expect, when he came home from work.

"Don't worry, I'm not going anywhere." Pat assured her.

Dolores lay down to sleep but she coughed and struggled for breath. Pat did her best to make her comfortable. She wanted to call the doctor but Dolores would have none of it.

"I don't want to be a nuisance. What a disgrace to have cancer. What a disgrace to Peru's family."

Pat said nothing. There was no love lost between her and her sister's husband and in-laws. She had always felt that Dolores had thrown her own life away to slave for people who showed her no love whatsoever. Now she was dying, nothing had changed. The cancer that was eating at her sister's throat was filling her lungs with pus, choking her and making it almost impossible to breathe. She had had a tracheotomy but still struggled to breathe and talk. Pat sat there holding Dolores' hand and she eventually settled into a fitful sleep.

Pat heard a car drive up and knew that Peru was home. She braced herself, hoping against hope that he would not be drunk. But she soon heard him in the kitchen arguing with his daughter, Ramini, who had been chatting with her cousin, Chandra, Pat's daughter. He was accusing her of running around with a young hooligan in the neighbourhood and she began crying. Chan, a chip off the old block, jumped into the fray and started defending her cousin.

"Shut your mouth," Peru yelled at Chan. "You're a bloody rubbish like your mother. You are teaching my daughter your ways." Pat's blood was boiling. How could they behave like that when Dolores was so ill? She was about to go into the kitchen and shut them up, when she felt a frail restraint on her arm.

Dolores's appealing eyes were on her. "Please, help me dress. I have to prepare my husband's dinner."

"Don't worry, Ramini has it all under control. Chan and I will help her dish up. Let me help you with your dressing gown. You can wait in the dining room."

The atmosphere at dinner was tense but nothing untoward happened until the end. Throughout the meal Pat had been seething because there was so little consideration for her terminally ill sister. There was also rancour at the insult that Peru had hurled at her and her daughter. She was determined to bottle it all up for her sister's sake but Peru put that out of the question. At the end of the meal, after all the dishes had been cleared away and they were waiting for Ramini to bring in the tea, he asked Dolores to pass him an ashtray. Dolores feebly pushed an ashtray towards him. Enraged, he picked up the ashtray and flung it back at her.

"Is that the way to pass me an ashtray? Pick it up and put it down decently in front of me," he shouted.

This was too much for Pat. "What the bloody hell is going on this house? Who is the invalid here? First you come in and start a yelling match with the children and now you ask a sick and frail woman to wait on you? What's the matter with you? Can't you see that she is ill?"

"Get out of my house, get out right now."

"Your house, your house," Pat's scorn was tangible. "My sister bought this house and everything in it."

She would have gone on but she felt the frail hand on her arm again and she swallowed hard. Then she picked up her bag and walked out.

Chan came running after her as she marched to her car. "That was completely uncalled for. Why do you always behave like this? No wonder people call us Bushmen." They got in the car and drove off. Pat had nothing to say to her daughter. If people called her a Bushman, it had nothing to do with the fact that her mother was Coloured. It had everything to do with the fact that she was not afraid to speak her mind. Why should she be submissive? Where had that got Dolores? Here she was dying and still not respected. At least she, Pat, respected herself and that was enough for her. She was sorry that Chan could not understand this. She dropped Chan off at her flat and went home.

Pat sat down with a cup of tea but couldn't get Dolores's intense need to be baptized out of her mind. She was not given to tears but couldn't help herself as she thought of her sister, on her deathbed, being denied her last wish. Her father, also a Tamil man, had been very different. He had had a crucifix in his room and had studied the Bible everyday of his life, just as he had studied the Vedantas, the Koran and African religion. And she had thought all Hindus were like him, without religious prejudices. She felt helpless in this situation and it was not a feeling that she could tolerate.

A few days later, Dolores, who could no longer speak, struggled with pen and paper to ask Pat if she had been to see Father Raymond about her baptism. In the midst of all the women sitting around singing *kirtans* and funeral songs, Dolores wrote, "They can't stop him."

Devaki came up and whispered in Pat's ear. "I went to see Father Raymond. He will be here soon." Pat was amazed. She hadn't approached the priest because she could not bring herself to ask him to involve himself in Dolores' little deceit. But Devaki hadn't hesitated. Pat's father had forbidden baptism to prevent his daughters' suffering and here was this Hindu woman colluding in the baptism of her sister, for the same reason. Pat found her own understanding of religion and compassion quite inadequate and she envied Devaki her ability to go beyond inhumane restrictions.

She indicated that Devaki give Dolores the news. Devaki whispered in the sick woman's ear and a beatific smile spread over Dolores's face. She no longer heard the droning around her and made Pat aware that there was something she wanted from under her mattress. Pat reached down and pulled out a rosary. Dolores took it in her hands and soundlessly began to pray. Pat looked around at the women in the room. They continued to sing. One or two noticed the rosary but ignored it.

Then the priest arrived. One of the elders of the family, a rather gaunt looking woman, stood up and challenged him. "Why have you come here? This is a Hindu home?"

"I understand that. I have only come to see Dolores and to pray with her. Will you allow me to pray with her?"

Devaki intervened. "The priest is only going to pray. He is going to join us in our prayers. There's no harm in that."

Pat looked at the priest with searching eyes. She couldn't believe that he had agreed to the subterfuge. He was going to do something distinctly dishonest. She turned to her sister, saw her shining eyes, and said to herself, *Perhaps it is dishonest, but it is right. I must learn to accept it as Devaki has.* She made way for the priest who came and sat by the bedside.

The elder who had challenged the priest indicated to the others that they should continue with the singing. They began chanting and singing again, even more loudly than before. Pat was ready to explode; then she realized that if they continued caterwauling as they were, they would not realize what was happening so she turned her complete attention to Father Raymond and Dolores. The priest was speaking quietly to the patient.

"Dolores, I understand your deep desire to be baptized. And God is listening to you. I am only his servant and I perform his commandments. Sometimes, circumstances are so difficult that I do not know how to proceed. In this case, the family into which you married believes that you must follow its customs and ways. Though you have done so all your life, I know that that is not what you want now. But as I told you, God is listening to you. He feels the yearning in your heart and He will do what I cannot. Speak to Him and He will grant what you desire."

She looked at the priest with questioning eyes.

"Pray now with me and you will feel His spirit enter into you and you will be baptized and blessed." Pat could hardly hear what was being said. The noise of the *kirtans* and the cymbals was drowning out the priest's words. But Dolores was listening intently and in her eyes there was clear understanding.

Father Raymond knelt down beside the bed. Devaki knelt on the other side. The singing of the women intensified. Pat took in the scene and suddenly felt impelled to kneel down beside Devaki. It seemed to her that a light enveloped them and nothing else existed in that room but the three kneeling figures and the woman on the bed. And Dolores, who had not been able to speak, raised her voice and clearly asked the Lord to bless her and take her into his care. She looked up and drops of water began rolling down her forehead. Devaki pointed in amazement and Pat stared in wonder. Dolores smiled and fell into a deep, comfortable sleep.

Suddenly Pat became aware of her surroundings again and she stared at the other women. The singing and chanting had continued unabated. They were not aware of any unusual happening. Had she been dreaming? She turned to Devaki whose eyes were filled with tears and they embraced one another. Father Raymond stood up and as Pat earnestly searched his eyes, he said, "She has been blessed." Then he shook hands with them and left.

That night the cancer, which had grown like a rotten potato on the side of Dolores's neck, burst and the stench of it overcame the camphor and the incense and sent all the singers scuttling from the room.

A month after Dolores's funeral, Pat went to see Father Raymond and was baptized into the Catholic faith.

Ghosts

Mrs. Marilele was watching her helper picking mangoes from the trees at the back of the house. She was hoping to earn a good sum from the harvest, which would be sold on the streets of Dzumeri. Soon her paw paws would be ripe and these would go out on the streets as well. She looked up into the avocados trees, bordering the mealie patch, but the fruit looked too small to pick just yet. She was quite dependent on the earnings from her garden. After the death of her husband, the Minister of Education in the old homeland, things had become very tight without his income. As the widow of the late Minister, people thought she was rich and expected her to maintain her former lifestyle in the big house in the affluent section of the township with a garden that flourished all year round despite water restrictions and frequent cuts. But she was a keen gardener and tended her plants with great care.

And she had practically replicated this garden at her school in Komanani Village. She became principal there after her husband was made Minister and knew what everyone thought, so she had had to prove that she had earned this promotion. On her first day at her dilapidated school, she had realised that her responsibilities would have to reach beyond, into the destitute village. And she took up the challenge immediately. She turned a large part of the school grounds into a garden and soon began supplying the villagers with fruit and vegetables. She also distributed second hand clothing that she collected, provided washing powder for children's clothes and used her bakkie to transport sick children to the clinic in the township. She did it all independently of everyone, including her husband, the Minister of Education.

She sighed as she turned to survey her five bed-roomed house. This big house was a cold and indifferent place, different from Komanani, where all the villagers knew and loved her. The sun was beginning to set, so she left her helper to put away the mangoes and went into the kitchen. Twenty years before, when her husband had taken up his post as Minister of Education, they had bought this plot and built a house that reflected his new status in the community. At the time, she had been a lecturer in Home Economics at the local tech, with a head full of ideas of her dream house. So she had put together the plan for their new home.

As she put the kettle on to boil, she looked around the kitchen. It was spacious and well-equipped with plenty of working surfaces. The wide counter that projected from the wall next to the electric stove, served as a sideboard when it was not being used for preparation of food.

Affixed to it at normal table height was another counter at which they used to eat breakfast. Of what use was it now?

Her kitchen had a gas, as well as an electric, stove because, like the water, the supply of electricity was quite erratic. She was an excellent cook and had needed a place in which she could demonstrate her expertise and dazzle the important guests that came to her house. Hers was one of the few houses in the area with an open hatch looking into the dining room. But after Marilele died, she lost interest in cooking, moved the TV into the dining room and watched listlessly as the children, they were young adults by then, drifted off, taking their meals in isolation in the kitchen, in their rooms or in front of the TV. They no longer dined as a family.

She made herself a pot of tea and sat at the counter. Why had she built such a big house? What an extraordinary extravagance! Her daughters had careers and were established in their own homes in other provinces. Only her son lived at home. Her mother was old, alone, and needed care, and she could have taken her in but her in-laws would have objected. So she had been forced to build a separate house for her at great cost to herself and was now financially responsible for two households.

She took her tea and went to her usual haunt, the big dark lounge where she sat alone in an easy chair. A huge framed portrait in the brightly lit passage dominated the room. From it, the handsome face of her deceased husband, in his Minister's robes, smiled proudly down on her. She often sat there for hours after school and well into the night, dreading the thought of that bedroom and that big bed where she would lie alone. At the age of fifty-three, she was still a beautiful woman and as his widow was always very smartly dressed. She knew her in-laws and the community were watching to see if she would take up with another man but she would never do that.

She had other ways to occupy her time. She was a dynamic woman and a staunch Christian and had become the chairperson of the Christian Women's Association at her church. On Thursday evenings, the Association met at her house for prayers and church business, especially funerals. There was a funeral practically every Saturday and the members were in and out of her kitchen, bringing huge dishes of biscuits, scones and other eats. With one or two committee members, she delivered the food to the home of the deceased's family so that they would have sufficient refreshments for all the people who would come to pay their respects. On the day of the funeral, she got all the members together to help prepare the meal and serve all those who had attended the obsequies. Funerals were very costly events and the Christian Women's Association, under her leadership, always provided solid support.

Perhaps it was because she was such a good organiser and everything she did was first rate, that people resented her. Her school for example, was well run and the envy of other schools in the area. So there were those who attributed her successes to her husband's influence and position and now that he was gone, wanted to see her fail.

As she sipped her tea, she suddenly went cold. She could feel that presence in the room again. Why did she keep coming in here? She had to get out. She would drive off in the bakkie and visit someone, anyone. But she couldn't move. A dark form was lurching toward her in a drunken stupor. As it loomed over her and reached out, she started out of her chair and choked back a scream. Why was he here? Why did he keep coming back? She tried to pick up her Bible and fling it at him but her hands were paralysed.

"What's wrong, Ma? You look like you've seen a ghost." She stared for a long moment. "Are you all right, Ma?" Jonah's face came into focus; he was the image of his father, just as Marilele had been when they were newly married. She quickly pulled herself together.

"Yes, I'm fine. What do you want?"

"Nyeleti is back and wants to see me. May I use your bakkie?"

She picked up her handbag from the floor next to her chair, scratched in it for a moment and then handed him the keys. "Make sure you lock up properly when you get in." She resented giving him the keys. She resented his presence in the house, this living image of her dead husband. He was her only son and her only failure. All the girls were doing exceptionally well. The oldest daughter was studying law, the second, graphic design, and her youngest, drama. She had already appeared in several TV advertisements and was being considered for a role in a soap opera.

But Jonah! He was a cross she was forced to bear. At university, he had got into bad company, started smoking dagga, became a heavy drinker and joined in all the boycotts of lectures, demands of "pass one, pass all" and money for bashes. He was a bright lad but he had failed all his courses and after two years had been excluded from the university. Now he was nearly thirty, without prospects, and had made no effort to find a job. He was a disgrace and she was ashamed of him. All he did was eat, sleep and watch television.

He was the son of the late Minister of Education and she wanted to kick him out. She gave a cursory glance at the portrait. She had tried, in many subtle ways. She had arranged for uncles to introduce him to prospective employers, had organised interviews for him, pointed out ads in the papers but nothing had worked. She had even begged her daughter, Tintswalo, to get him into television. After all he was a very handsome young man and what more did they need for TV? Tintswalo had tried but Jonah wasn't interested. He preferred to sit around doing nothing, sleeping away the days, drinking away the nights and in between drugging himself with television. She didn't know how to get rid of him.

She heard the bakkie returning. He was coming back with Nyeleti. Mrs Marilele couldn't understand how a nice girl like Nyeleti could get involved with a useless fellow like her son. Nyeleti was smart and had a good job in Pretoria. Why did she keep coming back here to this good-for-nothing? Were looks all that mattered to the girl? Although, Mrs Marilele referred to Nyeleti as his wife, she and Jonah were not married. Mrs Marilele had spoken to the girl many times about her relationship, trying to get her to end it. She couldn't see why Nyeleti should ruin her life being attached to a man like Jonah. And she looked up at the portrait. My God! What was that black blob clinging to the frame over his head? It was that bat again.

She had asked her cousin, Samson Ngobeni, who was building a garage to protect her bakkie from car thieves, to get rid of the plague of bats in her ceiling. He had come the night before when the bats were out feeding. She had ordered Jonah to assist Ngobeni and they had closed up all the holes and spaces under the eaves and the openings between the roof and ceiling so that the bats would not be able to get in again. In the process, a couple of ceiling boards in the passage were damaged. She blamed Jonah for that. That afternoon, when she was coming through the passage, a bat that had been trapped in the ceiling, fell through one of the broken panels, almost on top of her. She had screamed. Jonah had tried to catch it but it had flown off and he hadn't been able to find it. Now it was clinging, like an evil omen, to the frame of Mr Marilele's portrait.

When she heard Jonah and Nyeleti coming through the kitchen, she called out, "Jonah, that bat, it's back. It's sitting on your father's portrait."

She heard Nyeleti, "Bat! There's a bat in the passage? I'm going into your room until you get rid of it." She heard the door slam and then saw Jonah coming down the passage. He threw a cloth over the bat but the animal flew off before he could catch it and Jonah went scurrying up the passage after it. She waited and then called out. "Did you get it?"

"No, Ma, I can't see where it went."

She sighed. Then she heard Nyeleti. "You didn't get it?"

"No, it's hiding in the dark somewhere. Don't worry it won't come out now. Come on, let's watch *Generations.*"

That was their favourite soapie. Mrs Marilele couldn't understand how they could watch such trash. She never watched anything but the news. Just as she picked up her bag to go to her room, she heard a yell and the sound of running, followed by Nyeleti's screech of laughter. Then Nyeleti came into the lounge and collapsed on the sofa. She was laughing so hard she could hardly get the words out. "It's that bat. It was hanging there on the curtain and when Jonah tried to catch it, it fell behind the cabinet so Jonah left it there, said he would get it at the end of the programme. We sat down to watch again when Jonah suddenly jumped up, clutching his trousers high on the right thigh. He said, 'It's the bat. It's climbed up my trouser leg,' and dashed off to remove his pants." Nyeleti doubled up with laughter again. "The bat was only looking for a nice dark place to hide." Then Jonah, in a pair of shorts, clutching the trousers with the bat imprisoned inside, came to call Nyeleti. They went out to release the bat and Mrs Marilele went off to bed.

The next day, when she got home from school, her neighbour came over with an invitation to a party. She was surprised. She didn't go to parties and had not been to one in the five years after her husband's death. She immediately started to think of excuses but her neighbour wouldn't take no for an answer and left. She toyed with the invitation for a while. It was only her neighbour. Where was the harm in it? Really, her neighbour - how could anyone accuse her of being improper? She decided she would go - just for a little while. But that night she had a dream. She was at the party - it was a braai and all the men were in shorts. She was helping with the salads and cutting up bread. Then she walked over to the braai stand and was chatting happily when her husband suddenly appeared in front of her, cutting her off from the men around the braai. He stood there, eyes flashing with rage, not uttering a word. He took a step towards her and she put her hands up to defend herself but he was gone as suddenly as he had appeared. She woke up and sat there shaking in the dark. She couldn't go to that party.

The next evening, she stayed put in the dark lounge gazing at the portrait. The face had changed. The smile was gone and the eyes, crazed with rage, blazed down on her. She closed her eyes and tried to block out the visage but that only made things worse. She could feel him enter the room and she cried out in fear.

"Why have you come back? I am not going to the party. Get out. Leave me alone."

"Ma? Sorry, Ma, I didn't mean to disturb you."

She stared hard. " Jonah?" She pulled herself together. "What do you want?"

"Are you all right, Ma?" She didn't respond. "Ma..."

"What do you want?"

"Nyeleti has come for me, but if you're not well..."

"You don't usually ask for my permission."

"We don't have to go out. If you're not well..."

"Don't pretend you're worried about me. Get out! Leave me alone." He hesitated. "Get out!"

After he had gone, she became very restless. She reached for her bag and keys and went out through the kitchen. She hadn't visited her mother for two days; she would pop in there. She got into her bakkie and drove down to the main road. When she came to the stop, before she knew what was happening, her window was smashed in, her door opened and she was being pushed to the passenger's side. Suddenly, she found herself, wedged between two men in balaclavas, racing off down the main street and into the road leading to Komanani village.

She was frozen stiff. She said not a word. She knew she would soon be dead. When they got to a dirt road leading to Bambeni, the first village on the way to her school, they brought the vehicle to a stop. The hijacker with the gun opened the passenger door, jumped out, pulled her down and kicked her to the side of the road. She waited for the attack but the man jumped back into the bakkie and it disappeared into the night. Mrs Marilele alone in this dark, isolated place was dreadfully calm. She hadn't been raped. Thank God, for that. She could see dim lights from candles and gas lamps ahead and began to make her way towards them. But then she heard a car behind her. Her heart began to pound and she ran screaming toward the lights of the village, but the car pulled up alongside and in panic she hurtled forward, stumbled and fell. Kneeling there in the dirt, she waited again for the attack and prayed that the end would be quick. Then she heard someone calling out.

"Mrs Marilele, is that you? What are you doing out here alone?" The voice was familiar. It was Mr Risimati, chairperson of her School Governing Body. He got out of the car and helped her up. "Are you all right? What happened?"

She whispered hoarsely, "Hijackers."

Mr Risimati put her in the car and drove her back to Dzumeri. After she made her report at the police station, he took her home. His knocking woke Jonah and when he told him what had happened, Jonah looked shocked and very concerned. He quickly put the kettle on to make tea for her. Then he knelt next to her chair and put his arm around her. "Ma, I am so sorry." Involuntarily, she dropped her head on his shoulder and accepted his comforting presence. And for a moment she felt safe. But she jumped up suddenly.

"Don't pretend. You know exactly what happened. The hijackers are your friends. You planned this, didn't you?" She was glad to see pain in his eyes. "You wanted to punish me. But I did nothing wrong. I didn't go to that party."

Jonah looked shocked. "Ma, I think you should go to bed. You have been through a terrible experience. We'll talk in the morning." He tried to put his arm around her again to lead her to her room but she pulled away.

"Don't touch me, you drunken lout. Why do you keep coming here? You killed yourself and nearly killed me too. Dead drunk but you insisted on driving. I tried to stop you. Everyone thought the taxi driver caused the accident. But it was you, you, the big shot Minister. Go away. Get out. Don't keep coming back."

"Mother, please go to bed."

"Go to bed? Go to bed? To be groped by a drunken lout. No more! No more!"

"Mother . . ."

"Get out. Get out of my house. I never want to see you again." She burst into tears, ran off to her bedroom and locked herself in.

After a restless night, she finally fell asleep and stayed in bed until late the next morning. When she went into the kitchen, she found a letter from Jonah. She made a cup of tea and went to the lounge to read it. He had been in touch with the insurance company and given them all the necessary information. They were faxing forms for her to fill out and would replace her vehicle very shortly. He was sorry about what had happened to her and had finally realised that he could not continue to be a burden on her. Nyeleti was giving him a lift to Johannesburg where there were more opportunities and he was sure to find a job.

She dropped the letter and painful sobs constricted her chest. "He's gone. My husband. He's gone." When the spasms were over, she looked up at the portrait and all she saw was a vain man in ministerial robes. She stood up, pulled open the drapes and let the sunshine into the lounge.

Freedom Fighter

Elsabe peered through the screen door and saw Helen at the piano. She was always reminiscing about her days in musical theatre and had just finished singing, *Climb Every Mountain.* As Helen closed the piano, Elsabe heard David, "Thank you, darling, that was beautiful." Elsabe could smell biscuits; David baked every afternoon. They were very useful as neighbours. They kept Uhuru, her four year old, entertained when she was busy and that was nearly everyday. Helen fed him milk and biscuits and they played with the finger puppets that she made for her Grade 1's at the local primary school. Afterwards, David played football with him on the lawn and read him stories. They were like his grandparents.

Elsabe found him there every afternoon. She would have to do something about his habit of walking around the campus village knocking on doors looking for her. Sometimes he stopped at the Andersons where he played with their twins for a while. Sometimes he played with Mrs. Baloyi's children but Mrs. Baloyi did not like him because he made the children take off their underwear for his games. That woman didn't understand children's natural curiosity.

Suddenly, Uhuru spied her through the screen, jumped out of David's lap, ran to the door, unlatched it and leapt into her arms. He began crying loudly, "You left me. Why did you leave me? You said you were coming home. Why did you leave me?" This was his usual complaint. Elsabe tried to soothe him but he was too angry. She looked at David and Helen and shrugged. "I better take him home. He's very tired. We won't get any sense out of him while he's like this. Thanks for taking him in." She slipped out with Uhuru crying in her arms.

Elsabe lived just next door. As she was coming up the garden path with Uhuru, she could hear music and laughter issuing from her living room. Uhuru clung to his mother and cried bitterly. "Tell them to go away. I don't want them here. Tell them to go away." Elsabe sighed. It was tough being a single mother. It wasn't just her job; she was also a member of an underground cell. She walked in to find some of her students, stretched out on the bean bags and cushions, drinking beer, drawing on joints and talking about a comrade's narrow escape from the security police that day.

"Hey, Elsa, where you been, Comrade? Did Mr. Donkey stop you on the road?" Themba grinned at her over his beer. "That Mr. Donkey, he stands there in the road and he won't go." He called roadblocks Mr. Donkey.

Elsabe just smiled. She didn't have time for Mr. Donkey stories; she had to get Uhuru to bed. He was being extremely troublesome. He didn't want to stay in the bathtub by himself and each time she tried to join the others, he began screaming and crying. After she had bathed him and put him in his pyjamas, she had to lie down with him because he would not let her go. But, thank goodness, he was very tired and soon fell asleep. And she left him to join her companions in the living room.

She settled down next to Themba, took the joint from him and inhaled deeply. "This is good stuff."

"Specially imported from Tekwini." Vusi smiled. "I had to attend the Student Organisation's National Exec meeting in Durban last week and one of the comrades had stacks. This is compliments of SO."

"What's SO up to?" Elsabe enquired.

"Well, SO is organizing a nationwide school boycott. Workers and teachers must go on strike too. We will make the country ungovernable. You can forget about that assignment you set us, Elsa." Themba laughed as he opened another can of beer.

"That's what you think," Elsabe replied. "I am not about Bantu Education. My assignment is part of the struggle."

Themba pulled her close to him and gave her a deep and long kiss. "Now, do I still have to do that assignment?"

Vusi was annoyed, "Hey, Themba, don't talk rubbish." He turned to Elsabe. "What have you been up to today, Comrade?"

"I was at a meeting in the north. Comrade Bafana outlined a plan for setting up civic structures in this region. Then we went to Groot Krans to meet with comrades there who have already begun organizing. They should have their Civic Association set up by the weekend. Hey, we had a close shave in Groot Krans. While we were discussing our plan, the police came. They wanted to know what we were doing there. They looked at me suspiciously."

Themba smiled. "Yeah, one white face amongst all the Blacks."

"But then they began to scrutinize Bafana, so I quickly told them that I was a lecturer and all the others were my students and I was simply helping them with a research project. They frowned at me, so I showed them my dog tag from the Department of Education and told them they could telephone the Chief Minister. He would confirm that I am a lecturer at the College. They examined my card for a long time. They were very suspicious but decided to accept my word. Then they told us to get out of there. So we got up and left. Luckily, they didn't recognize Comrade Bafana. You know they're looking for him. But these were only the local police. They're pretty dumb."

'Bloody sell-outs. We should show this homeland government what we think of it. We should burn down the Chief Minister's house." Themba was excited at the prospect.

Vusi pulled deeply on his joint. "In Durban, they are saying that Mandela will be released soon. You know they've moved him from Robben Island to Pohlsmoor Prison. Just imagine it, 27 years in prison. Man, that's my whole lifetime. I was born in1963."

"I don't think I could have survived that long in prison." Elsabe shivered as she thought of it. Some of the people she had worked with, before she came here, were in prison. She was lucky; she had always managed to escape the security police. She was convinced it was because she was Afrikaans. She believed that the security police, who were mostly Afrikaners, had an innate respect for all Afrikaner women. Besides she had broadcast it widely that her father was a member of the Afrikaner Weerstands Beweging (Afrikaner Resistance Movement). She knew activists would be impressed that she had overcome her rabidly racist upbringing.

The telephone rang. It was Lars, a former boyfriend, a Swede who had long returned to his country taking with him their little son, Sven. Lars was not Uhuru's father. Uhuru's father, Martin Brown, had inducted her into the struggle. But he had left the city behind and was working in rural areas setting up cooperatives where poor Black rural women learned how to work together to develop viable businesses out of their indigenous crafts. Although they had separated some time ago, Elsabe had come to this remote part of the world so that Uhuru could be near his father. But Martin worked some distance away and had come to visit only once or twice and only at her request. Elsabe really wanted him to take responsibility for Uhuru in the way that Lars had taken Sven. She didn't have time to bring up a child. Elsabe was quite annoyed that he could not see that she was as much a freedom fighter as he and a child was complicating her life dreadfully.

"Lars, what a surprise," Elsabe returned into the mouthpiece. "How are you?" Lars informed her that he was fine and also indicated that Sven was doing well. "Oh yes, Sven. I am glad he's well." She listened again and then exclaimed, "His birthday! Oh, how could I have forgotten? Give him a big hug for me. He's what, seven, eight now?... Thirteen!" She couldn't believe it. "Is he really?" As she listened, she was beginning to lose her patience. "But this is not a good time. You know the situation in South Africa. The police have gone crazy and I am in constant danger." But Lars put the boy on the line and she had no choice. "All right then. At the end of the month." Lars came back on the line. She wanted to scream when he began giving her instructions and demanding assurances from her. "Don't worry," she interrupted testily, "I'll take care of him."

She almost banged the 'phone down. "Can you believe it? Sven is coming down at the end of the month."

"Who's Sven?" Themba took a swig from his can of beer.

"My son."

Vusi was surprised. "You have another child besides Uhuru?"

"Yes. It was a long time ago. I was very young. Lars was crazy about me. That's why he took Sven with him. It was a way of keeping me with him. Sven is thirteen. I haven't seen him for... my God, ten years. I barely know what he looks like?"

"You haven't seen him for ten years? Why is he coming now?"

"Going through some kind of teenage crisis. Wants to get to know his birth mother. I tried to tell Lars it's not a good time. He said he didn't actually want to send Sven but Sven was insisting. Listen, Themba, you'll have to go with me to the airport to fetch him when he comes."

"Themba doesn't have a car. I'll take you."

"No, Vusi, Themba will drive my car." Vusi swallowed looking resentfully at Themba, who smiled back at him expansively. Elsabe knew that they were competing for her affections. Not just Themba and Vusi, but all of them. They came here practically every night to imbibe and wait for when she would pick one of them. It was all very amusing. But right now she had a problem. "What the hell am I going to do with the kid? He won't fit in here. And where am I going to get the money to entertain him. Lars is only paying his airfare." It was bad enough being responsible for one child and now to have this one on his way too. She was mad; she had thought he was out of her life. She had even forgotten about him. She would have to find people to dump him with. But who?

"Don't worry," Themba drawled. "We'll take care of him. He's old enough. We'll teach him."

"You'll just get him detained. No, I'll have to think of something. Boys, it's time for you to go back to the hostel."

As the others stood up to leave, she took Themba by the hand and led him into her bedroom. She could hear thick exultation in Themba's voice as he called out, "Goodnight, comrades."

The next day, when Elsabe returned from her meeting with Comrade Bafana, she came straight to Helen and David and found Uhuru playing with toys on the living-room floor. As usual he jumped up and cried. She held him close in her arms but she didn't just leave, as she usually did. She knew that Helen was a very sympathetic woman and had decided to see how far her sympathy would stretch. She sat down and began to tell Helen and David about her troubles. They looked surprised when she told them of Lars and Sven. "I was very young when I met Lars, only seventeen. He was an international journalist; he swept me off my feet. We lived together for a while but he wanted to go back to Sweden, and that ended it all. How could I leave? My destiny is here, in the struggle for liberation. I couldn't go with him." She paused and sighed. "Now Sven wants to visit. I don't know what I'm going to do. I haven't seen my son for ten years but I don't have the money for his airfare." She hugged Uhuru closer. "Oh, how I curse my Afrikaner background. A poor farmer's daughter living on a remote farm, I have been severely disadvantaged."

David looked sceptical, "You lived on a remote farm? How did you meet an international journalist?"

"Through the struggle. Through the struggle, of course. But what am I going to do? I need at least two thousand rand for the airfare." She sighed again. She saw Helen looking at David who was frowning and almost imperceptibly shaking his head. Elsabe sighed again, very deeply. "I suppose I'll manage somehow." Elsabe hugged Uhuru and kissed him gently on the forehead. "At least I am here for Uhuru. I missed Sven's growing up - his father took him away when he was three. Well, what will be will be." Elsabe stood up, her features set like a tragic mask. "I know I shouldn't but I was wondering if you..."

David streaked past her to the door. "Well, Elsa, it's too bad about Sven. Goodnight." But Helen motioned Elsabe to sit down. She knew David was frantically shaking his head and gesticulating to Helen behind her back. His wife ignored him and he stalked out of the room.

Elsabe sat there, her face buried in Uhuru's neck. A surreptitious tear dropped from her eye. Helen took her hand, "Look, I have some money in the bank. My retirement savings. When we leave here, we will not be eligible for pensions. I don't need it now. I can lend you some of it."

Elsabe turned her beautiful face to Helen, her eyes full of pain and gratitude, "Oh, I couldn't... not your retirement money."

"Nonsense. I am quite prepared to make a short term loan."

"Oh, you are so kind. What would I do without friends like you? I promise, I'll pay it back by the end of the month."

Helen made out a cheque for two thousand rand. Elsabe, full of love and tenderness for Helen, hugged her and then disappeared clutching the cheque and Uhuru.

Two days later, when David was coaching cricket, she tapped on Helen's door again. She hadn't come to get Uhuru; she had sent him off to Martin in his place in the mountains. He had to take some responsibility for his child. Why should she be the only one? Elsabe's face was distraught and unhappy as she looked at Helen through the screen door. "Oh, Elsabe, what's the matter? Please come in." Helen quickly made tea and served it with some of David's biscuits. Elsabe munching on a biscuit, perused Helen's face with large, mournful green eyes.

"I don't know how to tell you this. You will think I am trying to take advantage of you. No, I shouldn't ask you. Forget it." She took a sip from her cup and reached out for another biscuit.

"Ask me what?"

She could see that Helen was concerned and felt sorry for her. So she began to tell her about the time that her father had gone crazy. "He tried to kill the whole family but we managed to escape. He walked all around looking for us, shouting and calling. When he couldn't find us, he...," she clenched her fists and swallowed, "he went out into the veld, put his shotgun into his mouth and blew his brains out." She shuddered from the effort of choking back her sobs.

Helen was shaking her head sadly. "You are an amazing woman. To have overcome that background? Look at you today. Fighting for democracy." She shook her head in admiration. "What do you want to ask me?"

Elsabe brushed it off but Helen persisted. Eventually, Elsabe was forced to admit, "I made a mistake the other day. I actually need four thousand rand. I have to purchase a return ticket for Sven. I know I shouldn't ask you, but I have nowhere else to turn."

Helen did not hesitate, "Well, I have the money. As I told you, it's for my retirement. It's doing nothing in the bank. It won't hurt to lend it out for a few weeks."

Elsabe's green eyes widened with gratitude. She gave Helen a big hug and fervently vowed, "I will never forget this. I promise you, you will have your money back at the end of the month." Helen pulled out her chequebook again and Elsabe left clutching another two thousand rand in her hand. That night she threw a big party at her house and all her students came. They partied into the early hours of the morning, whooping and singing and laughing.

A week later, Elsabe and Bafana drove down to Johannesburg to pick up Sven. Elsabe had dropped Themba in favour of Bafana, a much more suitable companion and clearly going places. In the expensive new leather jacket that Elsabe had bought for him, Bafana looked very handsome. He was tall, well-built and dynamic; a charismatic activist leader in this rural area. He didn't sit around telling inane stories about Mr. Donkey. He was setting up civic structures and organising people at grassroots level all over the region. He lived a cloak-and-dagger life and the danger surrounding him was an aphrodisiac. Elsabe was hooked. She clung to Bafana for dear life. And she was aware that he was flattered to have a beautiful white woman at his side.

At the airport, they waited together for Sven, Bafana holding the sign with Sven's name that Elsabe had made. Eventually, a tall, blond boy approached them. When Elsabe saw him she could not believe her eyes. She threw her arms around him and held him close, so close. She had expected a child and here was this gorgeous boy, almost a man. She held him so tightly and so long that he began to squirm. She let him go and started to shower kisses on him. He looked embarrassed and even frightened. On their way back to the homeland, she sat close to him in the back of the car. It was a long drive home, more than four hours. They made one stop at one of those highway service centres and moved on. She knew Bafana had many pressing engagements the next day and had to be back with the comrades. As they neared the township, they encountered a roadblock.

"Just be quiet." Bafana's voice was calm and imperative. "I'll handle this."

Fortunately, it was the homeland police. They shone their torches in the car and looked around suspiciously. They asked Bafana to open the boot. They poked around and wanted Bafana to open Sven's bag. They were looking for arms. Bafana spoke to them in the vernacular and after they had exchanged words, the police told him to drive on.

"What did they want? What did you say to them?" Elsabe's voice was thick with excitement.

"They are looking for arms. They wanted to open Sven's bag. I told them I was your driver and that I had brought you and your son home from the airport. I showed them the airline tags and said there was nothing in there but clothes. I told them they could speak to the madam; she is the wife of Major Van Wyk of the security police. He would be very upset to know that his wife had been harassed by the homeland police." Elsabe laughed, then threw her arms around him and kissed him. "So I am Mrs. Van Wyk?" She laughed again. Then she turned to Sven and told him all about Bafana's work and what a hero he was. When they got home, she hastily settled Sven in his room. Then she and Bafana disappeared into her bedroom.

In the next few weeks, she was riding around to meetings at all hours of the day and night. She had to be by her man, striving alongside him, facing the hazards with equal courage. She left Sven to find his own way and was delighted when she learned that Uhuru had taken him to Helen and David and they had organized a tea at which he had met some of the teenagers on campus. Thank goodness for that. Now that Sven had many friends, he wouldn't be a burden on her.

She was very busy and she saw very little of him. He had come to her office once or twice but she could never spare the time to just sit around nattering about inconsequential things. When she came home at night, he would come out of his room but she couldn't really talk to him, not with Bafana there. In the morning, she just had time to make coffee for everyone and when the domestic worker came, she handed over Uhuru and left. Several times when she brought a few comrades to the house, she would draw all the curtains, and they would plan their next protest action, usually a boycott of schools or a protest march. Before they left for some secret destination, if she saw Sven hanging around, she would tell him "We have very important work to do. If anyone comes to ask for me just tell them that I am at the College."

He always irritated her with his naïve question, "Will you be at the College?"

"You must not ask me things like that. It is very dangerous."

"I just thought I'd walk over and we could chat."

"Oh Sven! I told your father this wasn't a good time."

"He didn't want to send me. I forced him."

"Well, you should have listened to your father." And then she was off. Kids were such a burden, especially now in these exciting times. Rumours were flying that Mandela was going to be released soon and the security police had gone mad. Elsabe needed to be with Bafana more than ever now. If they picked him up, she wanted to be there with him, to shock and anger the secret police.

Then it happened, Mandela was released from prison. Bafana told her to go into hiding; he warned all the activists. But like everyone else, she was euphoric and began to celebrate. She sent her students out into the township and in no time, they had pupils pouring out of schools, roaming the streets in droves, overturning cars and attacking anyone

who looked like an *impimpi*. She went with them on defiance marches
to the government offices and joined them at night, when they burned
the houses of MP's. But her frenzy died down when the security police
began rounding up scores of activists and Bafana and his comrades were
picked up.

The day after they got him, army and police vehicles besieged
the college. Nobody could enter or leave. Police were crawling all over
the campus. And Elsabe knew they had come for her. She was waiting
for them but when she opened the door and saw them in front of her,
she froze.

"Are you Elsabe Viljoen?" She could only nod. They pushed
past her into the house and began ransacking it looking for evidence of
treason. She stood in the middle of the room, her eyes, large and
expressionless, staring abstractly. Uhuru, who had just woken up, came
running to her. She picked him up mechanically and clung to him like
a drowning person. A policeman barged into Sven's room and when he
stumbled out to see what was going on, Elsabe turned desperately to
him. Policemen, rifling through her belongings, surrounded her. She
felt Sven put his arms around her and she leaned against him, trembling
violently. Then he was wrapping a blanket around her. What would they
do to her? Oh God, what would they do? She had never been detained
but she had heard the horror stories. Would she be tortured, raped, killed?
The policemen tore through her possessions and began bagging things.
Couldn't they see that she was just a helpless woman, a mother with her
two sons?

Then a sergeant ordered her to pack a bag; she was to be detained.
She couldn't move. She felt Sven guiding her gently into her room and
helping her to dress. He packed a bag and took her back into the living
room. A policeman grabbed the bag and she screamed. When another
was about to grab hold of her, Sven waved him aside and took her to the
waiting police car. He helped her in and gave her a hug; she couldn't
respond. Suddenly, Helen was poking her face at her through the car
window, "Don't worry, we'll take care of Sven and Uhuru." She didn't
understand. She did not even see Sven or Uhuru or the neighbours
standing around the house talking in shocked whispers. As the car drove
off, she sat staring straight ahead of her, "How could this be happening?
Oh God, my life has come to an end."

Jail Birds

Gavaza is busy mopping and cleaning the cell for a new prisoner, one of these political detainees. *They don't put them in with the others. They keep them by themselves. Each one gets a cell, like in a hotel. Since they released Mandela in February, the jail is filling up with teachers and students. They have nothing to do, so they just make trouble.* Gavaza looks around the gloomy cell painted dark grey, with an open toilet cubicle and a drinking fountain next to the low wall. *They will bring a bed in here. Political prisoners are too good to sleep on the floor. Now I have to look after this one, the first woman to come here. Hai, extra work for me. Why do these people want to fight the government? They should keep quiet and mind their own business. Now I have to keep my eyes on this woman, make her clean the cell, make the bed and not do anything funny. Watch her in the shower; see if she's hiding anything in her bum.*

Simon, one of the warders calls and Gavaza goes into the charge office. Two white security policemen are there with the woman, small and skinny with grey hair. Gavaza wants to laugh. *What is this old coolie doing here? How did she get involved in all this political nonsense in a bantustan? So old and wearing shorts, hau, hau, hau! She is sitting there very quiet but she doesn't look frightened.* One of the security policemen shouts at Gavaza, "Search her bag. Look for papers and bring them to me." Gavaza looks at the cheap suitcase on the bench near the door and then begins to go through it. She sees a box of tissues. She goes through the tissues very carefully. She looks up and sees the woman watching her. There is nothing here. She turns over the clothes, looks through a book and blank foolscap sheets that are inside one of the shirts; looks through the rest of the clothes and can find no papers so she closes the bag. The security policemen, who have been talking with Mrs Van Zyl, supervisor of the female section, notice that she has finished and one of them orders Simon to lock up the detainee. Mrs Van Zyl, Gavaza and Simon accompany her to her cell. Gavaza wants to laugh again. How can this small *gogo* be so dangerous? *"Even I can kill her like a cockroach."* In the cell, Mrs Van Zyl sees that there is no bed and orders Simon to bring one in immediately.

When Gavaza returns with the woman's supper at five o' clock, she sees that the bed is in and the old coolie is sitting on it. She has put her bag on the built-in seat and the sleeping mat is on the floor alongside the bed. Gavaza gives the woman her supper: six thick slices of brown bread, two big fat sausages, half a tomato and a mug of coffee. When Gavaza comes back to collect the plate and mug, she sees that the coffee mug is empty and half a slice of bread and the tomato have been eaten. The sausages have not been touched. She is shocked. *What's wrong with this woman? Simon told her that security picked her up early in the morning and she hasn't eaten all day. And now to leave all this food on her plate! She thinks she's too good, eh? All right, she can starve then.*

When Gavaza takes the food back to the kitchen, the supervisor becomes worried. "Why didn't she eat?" Gavaza simply shrugs. She can't understand why her supervisor is making such a fuss. So what if the stupid woman didn't eat? But Mrs Van Zyl is going on about hunger strikes and inquiries into prison conditions and all sorts of rubbish like that. *I should have quietly put all that food in a bag and taken it home. That's what I'll do next time.* After her chores, Gavaza goes out to hitch a lift back to the village. When she gets home, just after 7 pm, she has to cook for the next day. She has a family to feed. She's up by four in the morning, and by 5 am is out on the road hitching again. It takes at least two hours to get to work. She is at the prison by 7 am. She goes to wake up the woman and orders her to make her bed. She loses her patience when she sees how the woman is doing it and shows her the right way. At first the woman resists and then she laughs and gives in. Gavaza doesn't think it's funny.

When Gavaza brings the broom, the woman stands to one side so Gavaza can sweep. *Who does she think she is? She's the one in jail.* Gavaza pushes the broom at her. "You sweep!" The woman looks a little confused and then takes the broom and sweeps. Gavaza is surprised to see that she can handle a broom. Then she tells the woman to go out into the yard to wash. The detainee sticks out her hand and says, "My name is Lutchmee." Gavaza backs away, stares at the hand and tells her not to waste time. *This woman has no respect. I am a police matron. They should give us uniforms. Not these overalls.* She watches as Lutchmee brushes her teeth. The water is boiling hot and she can scarcely rinse her mouth. She asks for a plug for the sink and Gavaza tells her to use the wrapping from the soap to block the hole. Then the woman washes the clothes she has been wearing. To shower, she pushes the button on the wall and the water shoots out from the built-in spout in a short boiling jet. She has to keep her hand on the button if she wants a continuous spray. But the water is boiling hot. Gavaza laughs to herself as she watches the woman running and jumping through the spurts. After she has showered, Gavaza sends her back into the cell and goes to help with the prison breakfasts.

In the kitchen, she finds Mrs Van Zyl fussing about what to feed the woman. She puts together a plate of porridge and coffee. *Just like in a hotel! These troublemakers get special treatment but people like her, who work and do everything they are told, are treated like dogs.* She takes the prisoner her breakfast and when she goes back for the plate finds that she has not eaten the porridge. "I can't eat this porridge. The milk or something has gone off." Gavaza smells the plate and wrinkles her nose. Again the woman offers to shake hands and repeats her name, Lunchy or something. Hey, these coolies have funny names. *Doesn't she know she must respect me? I am in charge of her.* She gives Lutchmee a contemptuous look, collects the plate and mug and goes off to the kitchen.

Mrs Van Zyl throws up her hands. The woman is not eating. She will have to report it to the station commander. Gavaza can't understand the fuss. Lunchy was toyi-toying against the government, now why are these Afrikaners so worried about her? They should be glad if she kills herself. But this is not her problem. At lunchtime, the plate comes back again almost untouched. Mrs Van Zyl sends for De Lange, the station commander, and Gavaza hears them talking. The station commander complains about having to cater for people with different backgrounds. What does the woman expect? That they should start cooking curries?

Later that day, friends bring a whole lot of supplies for the woman, biscuits, chocolates, juices and a bag of wool. De Lange is so pleased that he picks up the supplies himself and marches off to Lunchy's cell. One of Lunchy's friends, a tall white woman demands to see Lunchy and even though they all tell her she is not allowed, she pushes her way through and Gavaza has to run after her to try to stop her but the woman storms into the cell right behind De Lange. The kommandant is taken aback and stands open mouthed. Lunchy is glad to see her friend and gives her a big hug. It's funny to see this short black woman embracing this big white woman. As her eyes inspect the cell, the friend tells Lunchy that they have brought her embroidery and that puts a big smile on Lunchy's face. Gavaza is waiting to see what De Lange will do. She is afraid he is going to blame her. But he is just staring at the intruder and motioning her out. Then De Lange finds his voice and tells the white miesies she must leave but the miesies is very cheeky and the kommandant almost pushes her out. When they have gone, Lunchy starts laughing. Gavaza wants to know what is so funny and she says, "Rita is fearless. Nobody can stop her once she makes up her mind to do something."

The kommandant comes back. He is very pleased with all the food that Lunchy's friends have brought and tells Lunchy he is trying to get her transferred to another jail where she can get her own traditional food. Gavaza can see that Lunchy wants to laugh. *No respect, even for the kommandant!* Lunchy tells him she doesn't need special food, but they mustn't give her meat, she's a vegetarian. The baas shakes his head. She will be better off somewhere else. When he leaves, Lunchy looks through the parcels and then offers most of the food to Gavaza. *Hau! I can't take it. If they catch me I'll be in trouble. What's wrong with this woman? She doesn't want even her friends' food.* Then Lunchy takes the wool and a big piece of cloth from the bag that she was so happy to receive and shows Gavaza the embroidery that she is working on. Gavaza covers her mouth and laughs. She calls that embroidery. Sies! It is so ugly! Lunchy puts the cloth on the bed and says she is going to start working on it right away. Gavaza leaves shaking her head and laughing. She has to go and help with supper.

The next day, when Gavaza comes to Lunchy's cell, she gets the shock of her life. Lunchy has used some of the wool to make a line and has tied it from the window bars on one side of the cell to the window bars on the other. She has hung her towel, panties, bra, shirt and shorts on the line. Gavaza takes one look at this, covers her mouth and rushes out of the cell. She comes back within a few minutes with Simon who tells Lunchy, "You can't have this line." " Why not? I need it to hang up my washing." When Gavaza reaches up to pull down her clothes, Lunchy explodes.

" Don't touch my things!" Gavaza stops in her tracks; Lunchy seems much bigger than she thought. "Get out of here. I put up the line;

I will take it down!" Gavaza leaves with Simon but she is annoyed. *The stupid woman. Doesn't she know that they will get in trouble if the kommandant sees the line in her cell? If she doesn't take it down, I'll show her who's boss.* When Gavaza takes her lunch plate, she sees that the line has come down and she is relieved. But the woman is sitting there pulled up, not smiling and greeting her as she usually does. Gavaza doesn't mind; that's the way it should be and she thrusts the plate at Lunchy.

But the next day Lunchy is friendly again. She shows Gavaza all the supplies she has stacked up on the bench. She can't eat all this food and asks if Gavaza knows anyone who needs it. Gavaza looks at the bench covered with plastic bags of biscuits, chocolates and juices. *It's a lot of food but I can sneak it all out over a few days. The family will be pleased.* She tells Lunchy she will see. Then she hands over the plate of food. Mrs Van Zyl has been making a great effort to get the woman to eat and Gavaza waits to see what Lunchy will do with the half tomato, some chips, a slice of avocado, vegetable pickles and bread that she has brought. She is sure Lunchy is going to explode again. Such rubbish food! No meat, no pap! But Lunchy looks up with a big smile and thanks her. Gavaza is shocked. *She is thanking me? I would never give anyone food like that. Hau! She thinks I make her lunch. What a stupid woman!* She goes off shaking her head while Lunchy tucks in.

Over the next few days, all the parcels are cleared out and Gavaza's children and grandchildren are very happy with the treats that she brings home. Lunchy asks her about her family and her work in the prison. Gavaza doesn't respond at first but Lunchy keeps pressing and she begins to tell her about herself. Lunchy looks very surprised to hear that Gavaza has been working at the prison for ten years but only earns a hundred and fifty rands a month even though she works seven days a week from seven in the morning to five in the afternoon. Gavaza is fifty-nine years old and looks after women prisoners and does the washing. Her husband, in his sixties, works on a farm and earns a hundred rands a month. They live in the village of Boyi with their nine children, ranging from age nine to forty.

A week after she has been detained, Lunchy's lawyer comes to see her and Gavaza is very surprised when Lunchy asks her to come and meet him. He is Advocate David Mabasa. He greets Gavaza and shakes her hand and she makes a little curtsy as she greets him. Gavaza doesn't know why she has been called to meet the advocate. All she knows is that Lunchy is strange and she must expect such things from her. After the visit, when Gavaza takes her plate, Lunchy removes the serviette and is very pleased. She thanks Gavaza copiously. *Oh keep quiet, woman. What are you getting excited about? Potato chips, a tomato, a slice of avocado and two fish sticks! Maybe Lunchy is happy because Mrs Van Zyl put a serviette over the food. But she is acting as though I am treating her special. Me? She's mad. Why does she think I am doing special things for her? If it were up to me, she would get the same as the others.*

On the second Saturday, Mrs Van Zyl gives Gavaza a plug for the washbasin in the yard and Lunchy gives Gavaza a big broad smile and washes herself from the basin so that she won't get burned. At lunch time, Gavaza again brings avocado, tomato, fish sticks, boiled vegetables and a cup of tea. Lunchy starts to dance around like a mad woman singing, "Tea, tea, Gloria's tea." When she tries to take Gavaza's hand to dance with her, Gavaza pushes her aside and she falls on the bed laughing. Despite herself Gavaza laughs too. *The woman is mad. Who is this Gloria?* The next day, Sunday, Gavaza comes running in. The kommandant wants all the wool and the embroidery. According to Mrs Van Zyl, the Major from the security branch came last Thursday and saw Lunchy working on the embroidery. This morning he phoned and shouted at the kommandant who shouted at Gavaza and the warders and sent them to retrieve the embroidery and search the cell. The Major thinks Lunchy has papers and books in the cell. They don't find anything except some scraps that Lunchy uses to wrap her sanitary pads. They take the scraps and the embroidery and wool. Lunchy looks disappointed. *Well, she can't have privileges.*

That afternoon, Rita, that tall woman who pushed her way into the cell the week before, comes to visit Lunchy. Again Lunchy calls Gavaza to meet her visitor. Gavaza doesn't want to but this is a miesies and she feels obligated to shake hands with Rita and curtsy. Gavaza sees that Rita has brought a lot of parcels for Lunchy. After the visit, Gavaza brings lunch and when Lunchy sees the plate, her eyes grow big and she smiles. Gavaza sees a lot of vegetables, two baked potatoes, pumpkin, cabbage with cheese sauce, tomato, fish sticks and rice. *A lot of food* today but no meat. How can people eat like that? When Gavaza comes back later to collect the plate, she sees that it is almost empty but Lunchy hasn't eaten the rice. *Hau! But Indian people like rice.* Lunchy is sitting on the bed reading the Bible. *The Bible! But she is not a Christian!* Lunchy smiles and says her friend brought it.

The next day, Monday, Gavaza goes off to the kitchen leaving Lunchy washing in the yard. A few minutes later she runs back. Lunchy is still at the washbasin, "They want everything clean, clean. The Major is coming." Lunchy, towelling off, exclaims, "Again? That's the third Major in the last three days. What do they want?" Gavaza is mopping furiously. She can't trust Lunchy with the job today, not when the Major is coming. "This is Major from Security. You better watch out." *Lunchy acts like she doesn't care. But when Major van Wyk comes, she'll jump.* That afternoon, a Major comes to inspect the cell. It is not the Major from the security branch. Like the others, he asks Lunchy about the food. *Hau! Lunchy says it's fine.* He is there for a few minutes and then off to the cells of other political prisoners. Gavaza goes to the kitchen to fetch Lunchy's food and sees that it is almost like yesterday's, except there are no potatoes. *But that mad woman will like it.*

Before Lunchy can eat, a warder comes in and tells her that the doctor is waiting to see her in the charge office. "Why? I didn't ask for a doctor." "Come. Come. The doctor's waiting." Lunchy follows him and Gavaza goes out with her. Gavaza shakes her head. *First the majors, now the doctor. They keep on checking. We are not ill-treating the prisoners? Only security police do that. I wonder how Lunchy will like the doctor; he doesn't know how to talk. He only shouts.* Gavaza watches as the doctor rudely calls Lunchy and talks very roughly to her. Lunchy talks back and looks at him like he's a fool. Gavaza laughs to herself. Hey, that doctor didn't get it all his way today. After lunch, Gavaza finds Lunchy with the Bible again. Lunchy spends the rest of the day and the next day reading the Bible. *Good. Maybe, it will help her to stay out of jail.*

On Wednesday, Gavaza is annoyed with Lunchy. *She wants clean sheets. But it's been raining everyday. Can't she see that? She asked for clean sheets on Monday. Tuesday she asked for clean sheets again. And again today.* "What must I do? It's still raining." "Don't they have machines for washing?" "No, I do washing." Then she says, "The people here are mad, and you will go mad because you work for mad people." *Hau, she has no respect. How can she talk to me like that?* Then Lunchy tells the warder she wants to see the kommandant. *Hau, she is going to complain. I better find some sheets.* Gavaza goes off to the laundry, looks through the cupboards, eventually finds some and takes them to Lunchy. She leaves when Lunchy goes to wash and because she is quite disturbed about the sheet incident, forgets to stay and lock her up and doesn't realise that she has given Lunchy extra time in the yard until one of the white policemen shouts at her. He had been to see why Lunchy wanted to talk to the kommandant and found her lounging against a wall enjoying the sunshine. Then Gavaza receives a phone call and rushes off because her daughter is ill. She is glad she didn't see the kommandant.

When Gavaza comes in the next morning, she is surprised to see Lunchy wearing a sleeveless shirt. 'Why you dress like that? You want to get sick? It's cold and raining." When Lunchy says, "I have hot flushes," Gavaza frowns and looks about the cell. *What is she talking about? I don't see anything.* Lunchy asks Gavaza about her daughter. Gavaza tells her she had an upset stomach but she's all right today. Gavaza's nine children all live at home. Six of them are working but make no contribution to household expenses. Lunchy wants to know why she hasn't kicked them out. *Hau! What kind of question is that?* So Gavaza retaliates, "And *your* children? Who look after them now." Gavaza is shocked to hear that Lunchy is not married and has no children. Gavaza shakes her head. *Not married. No children. What kind of woman is this?* "You looking for man?" Lunchy laughs, "What for?" Gavaza shakes her head. *You can't trust women who are not married. They are evil.* After lunch, Gavaza comes to release Lunchy so she can have her afternoon wash. "You hurry up. Security Major coming just now. You put on nice clothes." "Why? He's not my boyfriend?" Gavaza laughs. But the Major does not come.

Friday, while Lunchy is showering, Gavaza can no longer stand the sight of her ugly legs. "Your legs are grey. Why you don't put lotion on your legs." "I don't have any." "Buy some." Lunchy just looks at her. "Ask the policeman to buy for you. Write note and give him." Lunchy is surprised. "I don't have money." She really is stupid. "Didn't they take your money when they bring you here?" "Oh, I forgot about that. I had twenty rands on me. You mean they will let me have it? Oh good.

Bring me a pen and paper." "Ask warders. They give you paper, they give you money." The next day, Lunchy dances up to Gavaza and pulls her skirt up to her knees and shows off her legs. "Thank you Gavaza. Now I can enter a beauty competition."

On Sunday, while they are making the bed, Lunchy asks Gavaza if she is ZCC (Zionist Christian Church) and if she is going to Morea next weekend. "Easter not next week. Not for two weeks." "Oh good, my brother is coming next week. I thought he would be caught up in the Easter rush to Morea. I was going to tell the lawyer to tell him not to come." As she is tucking the blankets under the mattress she says, "Today is Sunday. Don't you go to church?" Gavaza puts her hand to her heart. "How much it hurts me. I can't go to church. But I worship at home . . . You too, you better pray in here." Gavaza is shocked to hear Lunchy say, "I don't have to. I am not a Christian." "You don't believe in Jesus?" "No." Gavaza wants to go down on her knees right there and then. Instead she orders the heathen out to wash, hurries her and locks her in so she can't spend any time in the yard.

Later that day, Lunchy is still going on about church. "Why don't you ask the station commander to give you leave to go to Morea? Isn't Easter the most important time for Christians?" Gavaza frowns and snaps at her, "They don't give time for church." Lunchy persists, "At least you have a service here then?" Gavaza shakes her head in frustration and walks out. *Lunchy has funny ideas. Church service in a police station? What next?* That evening, as Gavaza is leaving to go home, Simon tells her, "That Lunchy, she sent for the kommandant and told him you are a Christian and he must let you go to church on Good Friday. He didn't like that. He told her that you are a policeman and policemen are on duty twenty-fours hours a day. Then Lunchy asked him, 'Do you go to church on Good Friday?' De Lange went red. He was so angry. He told her he is the kommandant and this is his police station. She mustn't tell him how to run it. I could see Lunchy was worried. She told him not to blame you. You don't know what she is asking him. You know nothing about this. But the Kommandant just turned and walked out. I think he went to call the Major." "The Security Major? Hau, hau, hau! That woman is a troublemaker. Why doesn't she mind her own business?"

The next morning, when Gavaza comes to work, she is kept waiting. By the time a warder opens up Lunchy's cell, she is fuming.

She has been waiting since seven for them to open up. As she is going into the cell, someone calls to her to come and help with breakfast. She shouts back, "I'm busy." She tells Lunchy, "They don't treat me right. They tell me, so many time, I am old. I can't work nice. Hau, yesterday Mrs Van Zyl, she come in the yard and she take her finger over the floor like this, then she hold up finger and say, 'Look at this dust. You too old.' Today, I'm not going to help for the breakfast. If they shout, I'm going to tell them they must pension me off. Then they will keep quiet. They don't want to hear that." Lunchy says, "Good. We Black women must stand up for our rights." *What does she mean, 'we black women'?* For the rest of the week, Gavaza finds the Kommandant, Mrs Van Zyl and other white personnel rather abrupt with her. She is given extra duties and has to stay on past five o' clock. On one occasion, Mrs Van Zyl asks her, "You looking for trouble with the Security police?" Gavaza is shocked. *Did they report me to the Major? Hau, hau, hau! It's all that Lunchy's fault. She is a stupid woman.*

On Saturday, Gavaza receives bad news and is very upset. Lunchy wants to know what's wrong. Gavaza doesn't want to talk to Lunchy; she is in trouble because of her. But Lunchy persists and Gavaza needs someone to talk to. "Yesterday, my brother, he die. He only forty years. After he get money in bank, he collapse. He give his wife money and she put it in the pocket, then he fall down dead right there in bank. Why she put money in pocket? She put money in pocket and she kill him." Lunchy gives Gavaza the change from her twenty rands so she can visit her brother's family. Gavaza puts the nine rands in her pocket. *She mustn't think she can butter me up.* Soon afterwards, Gavaza comes back to tell Lunchy that her brother is here. Lunchy is very happy. She has been worrying about him. Gavaza knows he went for a big operation and is not so well but he has come all the way from the big city, all the way here to the north, four hours driving. *She is lucky to have her brother. My poor brother, to die so young.* Gavaza doesn't go to the front office when Lunchy's visitors come. She is too sad. When Gavaza takes Lunchy her supper, just a mug of coffee - that's all she ever asks for - Lunchy gives her some of the food her brother has brought. It is delicious; Gavaza enjoys the roti and curry.

On Tuesday morning when Gavaza comes to the prison Simon tells her, "Major van Wyk was here last night, with his partner. They came to see Lunchy." Gavaza can't control her anxiety. "The Major! Did he ask about me?" "I don't know. They took Lunchy into that little office there. They talked to her for a long time. I hear the Major talk, talk, talk. Lunchy, she didn't say much but she was arguing. They coming back tonight." Gavaza rushes off to see Lunchy to find out what happened. *Did the Major say anything about me?* She finds Lunchy sitting on the bed frowning. "So Major Van Wyk come to see you. What he say?" Lunchy looks like she is not going to talk. *It must have been bad.*

Then Lunchy says "Oh he had a lot to say. First he took out his gun and put it on the desk. Then he said, 'I do not wish to hear any sarcastic remarks from you or I will keep you in detention for as long as I like.' Then he told me I was one of those who organised the stay away in Gazankulu. I said I was not but he didn't believe me. So I told him, 'If you don't believe me, why are you talking to me. Send me back to my cell.' Then he said, 'I am a Christian.'" "You didn't tell him you not Christian?" "I didn't but I am very glad I am not. He said, 'I go down on my knees every night and thank God that there are cowards in this world." So I asked him, 'Are you calling me a coward?' He said, 'You are afraid and ashamed of what you have done.' 'No I'm not. But I won't confess to things that I have not done.'" "Yes, yes, but what he say about me?" Lunchy looks puzzled. "What he say about me?" "Why would he ask about you?" "He didn't ask? That's good. But he's coming back tonight?" Lunchy nods. "Maybe he will ask tonight." "Why? What have you done?" "Me, nothing. It's you. You tell the kommandant to send me to church." Lunchy bursts out laughing. "Yes, that is a crime isn't it?" Gavaza shakes her head. *Lunchy is crazy.*

The next morning, when Gavaza comes in Simon tells her, 'Hau, you should have been here last night. The Major, he was so angry. When they come out of the little office after interrogation, he look like a tomato. He shout at me to take Lunchy back to her cell. Then he ask about her embroidery and Lunchy smile and say, 'Oh, you took that already.' Then the Major ask, 'What you got to read?" Lunchy's smile get bigger and she say, 'The Bible.' The Major say nothing; he just march out. His assistant is dancing around. He look like he want to box Lunchy's ears." "What they say about me?" "I don't know. I didn't hear what they were talking inside."

When Gavaza goes into the cell, she finds Lunchy happily

snuggled in bed. "Get up, get up. We must make the bed and then you
must wash." Lunchy drags herself out of bed and helps Gavaza make
it. "What happened last night? What did the Major say?" Lunchy smiles.
"He asked me about you. He wanted to know if you belong to the
Christian Women's Association. He said he knows that the Christian
Women are planning to blow up the police station." Gavaza's hand shoots
up over her open mouth and she stares wide-eyed at Lunchy. *They can
fire me now and I won't get pension.* Lunchy quickly says, "No, no. I
am only joking. The Major didn't ask about you. He wanted to know
about the celebration I organised when Mandela was released. He wanted
to know about the Youth Group and the teachers' group and mainly he
wanted me to give him names so he can go and arrest people and put
them in jail." "He didn't ask about me?" "No, no. Anyway, why should
he arrest you? You're already in jail." "What you mean? I am a police."
Lunchy takes her towel and goes into the yard. Gavaza follows her.
"Why he so angry? Simon tell me he very angry." Lunchy laughs, "He
kept on calling me a liar so I jumped up and banged so hard on his desk,
his gun almost fell off. I told him I'm not giving him names. He got
angry because I was rude to him." Gavaza can't believe that Lunchy
would dare to shout at the Major. *They mustn't blame me for that. This
woman has no manners.*

On Good Friday, Gavaza arrives late and is very cross. She has
more duties because some of the other matrons haven't come to work.
She tells Lunchy she is not going to do the extra work. Lunchy stops
sweeping and leans on the broom to listen. Gavaza says, "Go on, sweep!"
Lunchy replies "Yes, baas," and springs into action. Gavaza laughs.
Then she tells Lunchy that this morning, she called Mrs Van Zyl by her
first name, Hannelie. "Mrs Van Zyl look up with big eyes and ask 'What
happen to 'miesies'?' I ask if 'miesies' is her name and Mrs Van Zyl
give me a dirty look and say, "Ja." Lunchy laughs and tries to shake
Gavaza's hand but Gavaza doesn't allow it. On Sunday, when Gavaza
takes Lunchy's plate, she greets her in Tsonga. Simon, who is Shangaan,
has taught Gavaza how to greet in Tsonga. Lunchy is pleased and tries
to answer but she can't understand what Gavaza is saying. She laughs
with Gavaza and tells her, "You have learned more in one morning than
I have in two years. But now I have plenty of time to learn and you can
teach me."

After lunch, a security police officer comes in and asks Gavaza to take him to Lunchy's cell. He tells Lunchy to pack her things; she is going home. Lunchy can't believe it. Surprised and excited, she turns to Gavaza who is standing there, a policewoman on duty. She doesn't look at Lunchy. *So Lunchy is going home. That is how it has been with this lot of detainees. Keep them for twenty-eight days and then send them home. The security they don't tell us anything. They just come and go, as they like. They bring these people, dump them on us and we have to look after them. Just when you get used to one, they take her away.* Lunchy, who is packing quickly, keeps looking up at Gavaza who ignores her attempts to communicate. Gavaza looks at all the parcels still piled up on the concrete bench. Lunchy says to the officer who is watching and waiting, "I don't want this stuff. I would like Gavaza to have it." He shrugs. Lunchy asks Gavaza to take all of it and the stuff in the fridge. Then Lunchy picks up her suitcase. "This is so sudden. I can't believe I'm going home. Goodbye Gavaza. Thank you for all your kindness. I will never forget you." Lunchy tries to hug her but Gavaza fends her off. Then Lunchy goes with the officer and Gavaza sighs with relief. Now she can go back to her usual routine without having to baby-sit anyone. *Hey, they mustn't bring any more political prisoners! They take too much advantage.*

Glossary

Annè -   Big brother (brother-in-law)

Athè -   Aunty

Atteridgeville - An African township

Bakkie -   Open van

Baas -   Afrikaans for Boss

Bhajan -   A congregation that chants and sings hymns

Bhajia -   Little spiced, fried balls made of chickpea flour

Braai -   Barbecue

Caffy -   (Colloquial for cafè)

Eersterus -   A 'Coloured' township

Gogo -   Grandmother

Gopuram -   Entrance tower/gateway of a Southern Indian style temple

Goolgoola -   Fried doughballs

Impimpi -   Sell-out, traitor

Inyanga -   A high priest of the African religion

Karma -   Action, commonly believed to be connected with ignorance (evil)

Kirtan -   Hymn

Koran -   The holy book of Muslims

Machenie -	Beerhall
Mamè -	Uncle
Miesies (Mrs) -	Colloquial for madam (employer)
Murthi -	Holy image, statue
Muti -	Traditional medicine
Parti -	Grandmother (Tamil)
Poosari -	Tamil priest
Pur -	Pastry for samoosas
Roti -	Indian round, flat bread
Samoosa -	Triangular pie
Saulsville -	An African township
Shangaan -	Tsonga, the language of the Tsongas in Limpopo Province
Sinuppa-	(Literally, small father) Uncle, father's younger brother
Tabla -	Drum
Tala -	Rhythm
Tekkie -	Canvas shoe
Umma -	Mother
Unni -	Sister-in-law
Vadè -	Spicy, fried flat cake made of crushed yellow split peas
Varaluxmi -	The goddess Luxmi who grants boons (vara)

Vedantas -   (Upanishads, end of the Vedas) - the holy scriptures
                  of the Hindus

Yegyim (havan) - The fire raising ceremony, a purification ritual

Yetoo -   Eighth day ceremony after the death of a family
                  member. It allows the family to resume their normal
                  daily activities. Neighbours and relatives have provided
                  for the family since the death.

Printed in the United States
by Baker & Taylor Publisher Services